Also by Alyson Noël

FOR TEENS

THE BEAUTIFUL IDOLS SERIES
Unrivaled

THE SOUL SEEKERS SERIES
Horizon
Mystic
Echo
Fated

THE IMMORTAL SERIES
Everlasting
Night Star
Dark Flame
Shadowland
Blue Moon
Evermore

★

Cruel Summer
Saving Zoë
Kiss & Blog
Fly Me to the Moon
Laguna Cove
Art Geeks & Prom Queens
Faking 19

★

FOR TWEENS

THE RILEY BLOOM SERIES
Whisper
Dreamland
Shimmer
Radiance

FIVE DAYS OF FAMOUS

ALYSON NOËL

Delacorte Press

Text copyright © 2016 by Alyson Noël, L.L.C.
Jacket art copyright © 2016 by Mina Price

All rights reserved. Published in the United States by Delacorte Press, an imprint of Random House Children's Books, a division of Penguin Random House LLC, New York.

Delacorte Press is a registered trademark and the colophon is a trademark of Penguin Random House LLC.

randomhousekids.com

Educators and librarians, for a variety of teaching tools, visit us at RHTeachersLibrarians.com

Library of Congress Cataloging-in-Publication Data
Names: Noël, Alyson, author.
Title: Five Days of Famous / Alyson Noël.
Description: First edition. | New York : Delacorte Press, [2016] | Summary: Relates the adventures of eighth-grader Nick Dashaway, whose Christmas request does not go according to plan.
Identifiers: LCCN 2015027454 | ISBN 978-0-553-53796-3 (hc) | ISBN 978-0-553-53797-0 (glb) | ISBN 978-0-553-53798-7 (ebook)
Subjects: | CYAC: Wishes—Fiction. | Christmas—Fiction. | Junior high schools—Fiction. | Schools—Fiction.
Classification: LCC PZ7.N67185 Kj 2016 | DDC [Fic]—dc23

The text of this book is set in 12-point Caslon.
Interior design by Ken Crossland

Printed in the United States of America

10 9 8 7 6 5 4 3 2 1

First Edition

For Irene, in loving memory of Bill

The two most joyous times
of the year are Christmas morning
and the end of school.

—Alice Cooper

PREFACE

(aka The Big Fat Lie I Told Myself)

Ever have one of those days when you just knew that, by the time it was over, you'd never be the same?

Only, in a good way?

For me, today was that day.

From the moment I woke up, I knew it was true.

Less than fourteen hours later, I fell for the absolute worst, most dangerous lie of all: the lie we tell ourselves.

If even the smallest smidgen of it hadn't been a lie, I wouldn't have ended up here—held hostage—on a runaway psychedelic Christmas Trolley—with a deranged Santa at the helm.

Which is how I know the whole thing was nothing more than a big fat delusion from the very beginning.

"On, Dasher! On, Dancer!" the lunatic shouts, one hand gripping the tinsel-wrapped steering wheel, the other waving wildly, as though wielding a whip on an imaginary herd of reindeer. The opening of "It's the Most Wonderful Time of the Year" blares from the overhead speakers as the trolley thrashes from side to side, under constant assault from a blizzard hurling snowflakes the size of golf balls. The strings of twinkling Christmas lights swing precariously overhead as sprigs of holly and mistletoe and random ornaments unhitch from the walls and career across the aisle.

"Better hang on tight!" The driver swivels toward me, the only passenger on board—the only one stupid enough to get on board—his long white dreadlocks flailing over his shoulder, his golden teeth gleaming, the spiral lenses on his glasses spinning so quickly in and out of focus they're making me dizzy. "This storm's about to get crazy!"

Only, when he says it, it sounds like *"Dis stawmsaboutagit craaazy!"*

I press my face against the window, pounding the glass as I frantically search for someone to help me, get on a cell and report this kidnapping in progress. But the snow is coming down so hard and fast, it's impossible to see much of anything. So I hunker low in my seat and check my own cell phone. No service. Same as before, when I was waiting for the normal bus to take me home.

But the note app still works, so I fight to steady my hand and thumb-type everything that took place, exactly as I experienced it, from the moment the trouble started until the moment I decided it was a good idea to accept a ride from a mental hospital escapee.

That way, when my body is eventually discovered, not only will the authorities have someone to prosecute, but my family will rest a little easier, knowing the whole truth behind the unfortunate chain of events that brought me to this dreadful conclusion.

It's the only thing I can do.

I'm pretty sure I won't live long enough to regret this.

DECEMBER 19
10:39 A.M.—11:50 A.M.

SPARKLE FIT

Today is the day my entire life changes for the better.[1]

And yet, as many times as I've gone over it in my head, it's still kind of weird to think that in just a little over an hour I'll have made the transition from Brainiac Nerd to the coolest guy in school. And the crazy thing is—for someone who's facing such a huge, monumental event—I'm not even nervous.

I guess it's like my hero, rock star/actor/singer/model Josh Frost, always says: you can't live it if you don't fully imagine it.

---

[1] The deadliest Big Fat Lie of them all—the one that kick-started this mess.

Well, I've spent the last year and a half fully imagining it, and it begins with the way I sit in this chair.

If it seems like something that simple couldn't possibly matter, trust me: when it comes to other people's perception—and by "other people," I mean seventh-grade girls—there is no detail too minor.

Seventh-grade girls, especially the popular ones, notice *everything*. And they can be pretty brutal with their assessments.

If you want to be noticed—and even better, accepted—then you need to wear the *right* jeans and the *right* sneakers (but you'll probably want to stop calling them *sneakers*), and you definitely need the *right* hair, which is basically styled to look as though you barely ever think about it, even though the time spent making it appear as though you barely ever think about it forces you to wake up half an hour earlier so you're not late for school.

And yeah, you even need to sit the right way, which is pretty much the opposite of how I usually sit, with both feet on the floor, my back mostly straight—you know, the way teachers and parents sit.

But no more.

Today I push my chair away from my desk and slide all the way to the edge of the molded plastic seat until my jeans pockets are hanging off the rim and my legs are stretched out before me. Once that's accomplished, I flick a hand through the hair I pretend to barely ever think about and covertly turn to my left like I'm only trying to brush my bangs from my eyes, when really I'm sneaking a glance at the far side of the room, where perfectly perfect Tinsley Barnes is too busy focusing on equally perfect Mac Turtledove to notice me looking so cool.

Still, I hold the pose way past the point when my butt starts to go numb, knowing that at any moment Tinsley could accidentally shift her attention away from Mac long enough to see the way I'm owning my chair and fall madly and deeply in love with me.

Only she doesn't.

But really, it's not a big thing.

So what if Tinsley's still under the illusion that Mac Turtledove is the only guy worth noticing?

It won't be long before she discovers she was entirely wrong about me.

Until then I just play it cool. Crossing my legs at the ankle, keeping it casual and loose, I shift my focus to the front of the room, where Mr. Sparks struggles with a tangled glob of tinsel that looks fat and promising until he climbs on top of his chair and tosses it over the chalkboard and it turns out to be as skinny and bald as he is.

But it's not like that stops him from folding his arms over his chest and admiring his work. His eyebrows rise in a question that's not really a question when he catches me watching, but all I can do is shrug in return.

He may be my third-favorite teacher (not my fault he doesn't teach math or science), but I can't fake enthusiasm I don't really feel. I mean, it's the last day of school before winter break—clearly he's a little late with the holiday cheer. Besides, with our test papers turned in and class nearly over, any authority Sparks may have held is long gone.

Pretty much everyone around me is deep into texting, gaming, goofing off, or, in the case of Tinsley Barnes and Ivy Wilburn, laughing hysterically at everything Mac Turtledove says as he slouches low in his seat like his butt is not at all numb and it's no big thing when the two hottest girls in the entire seventh grade pretend that you're funny.

In less than an hour, they'll be laughing with me—only they won't be pretending!

As I watch Tinsley swing her long blond hair—the color of hot, buttery, movie-theater popcorn—over her shoulder, I'm fully imagining how it'll be when she's standing before me, hair shimmering and bouncing, blue eyes sparkling, laying a soft hand on my shoulder and saying, "Oh my gosh, Nick, I had no idea you were *so* funny!"

"Look at that." Dougall Clement leans toward me, yanking the cord at my neck until my earbuds pop from my ears.

"Trust me, I'm looking," I say, unable to keep the grin from my face, sure he's talking about Tinsley and Ivy. I mean, other than Sparks's little chair stunt, there's nothing worth watching.

"Even Sparks can't escape it." Dougall frowns, shaking his head as he glares at the pathetic strand of tinsel dangling from the chalkboard.

I look at Dougall's squinched-up brown eyes, clueless as to where this is going. "You seriously protesting Christmas?" I ask, remembering the time, not long ago, when Dougall had to print his wish list in an eight-point font just to keep it within his dad's one-page limit.

Dougall looks at me like *I'm* the one not making sense. "I'm talking about the *bell*." He puts extra emphasis on *bell*, as though that alone clears up the confusion. "Look." He wipes a hand over his chin, growing increasingly frustrated. "The bell's gonna ring in, what—fifteen minutes?"

My eyes track the clock. "Nine," I say. I can't believe he didn't know that.

"Yeah, and because of it, Sparks goes on a sparkle fit, totally oblivious to the fact that no one even notices, because they're all in a trance waiting for a stupid bell to ring."

"And your point is . . . ?" I drag out the words, still not getting why he's so worked up.

"My point is, ever since the first day of kindergarten, our lives have been spent either waiting for a bell to ring or reacting to a bell that's already rung." His eyes sharpen. Lips flatten. Conspiracy Face—it's a look I know well. "So far, that makes for a steady eight-and-a-half-year stream of morning alarm clocks, start bells, end bells, break bells, lunch bells, final bells . . ." He slides toward the edge of his seat, forcing the folds of his bulky red sweater to bulge over his desk. "And we've still got five and a half more years to go, not counting college."

He cocks his head and squints into the distance as I fumble with the cord at my chest, straining to hear the Josh Frost song bleating from the speakers while mentally rehearsing the corresponding moves.

"Point is, they've got us right where they want us. Like Pavlov's dogs, we're completely programmed. And most of these people are too zombified to notice." He shakes his head as he flicks a disdainful look at our classmates. All of whom, much like me, are living for the moment the bell will announce our escape.

I drum my fingers against my desk. I have no reply. Unlike Dougall, I've got no beef with the system.

On any other day I'd probably go along—might even help build on his theory. But today, well, let's just say that today that bell is my friend.

The second it rings we'll make for lunch and then over to the school gym, where Josh Frost—International Superstar, with his very own reality show, *Frost World*—will judge the Greentree Middle School Talent Show.

The kid who wins not only gets to stand on the stage next to Josh, but he'll also snag an appearance on Josh's show, which is pretty much a fast-track pass to a much cooler life.

Luckily for me, I've fully imagined a routine that virtually guarantees the win will be mine.

From the second they announced that Josh was stopping by his old school to offer us a brush with fortune and fame, I knew it was just what I needed to rid myself of the unfortunate Brainiac Nerd label my classmates have given me.

If there's one thing I've learned since starting middle school, it's that the things that worked for me in sixth grade are now working against me.

I'm desperately in need of an image makeover.

Dougall is too.

But it's not like he's noticed.

He just slouches against his desk, shaking his head and sighing like an old man with two bad knees and a long list of regrets.

Dougall practically lives for conspiracy theories. Unexplained mysteries, Bigfoot, UFOs, the Bermuda Triangle—they're like catnip to him.

"We should start a revolt. Take back the clock." He nods like he means it but otherwise doesn't make a single move from his seat.

Dougall's a talker. A thinker. More into theory than action. He's also been my best friend going all the way back to the third grade, when he and his dad moved into the house next to mine and we discovered a mutual interest in getting good grades and avoiding PE.

But lately I can't help but wonder if Dougall might be holding me back.

He hasn't made a single adjustment since we got to this place.

And now, two years later, the only difference he sees between grade school and here is the number of bells.

He definitely hasn't noticed that girls no longer have cooties.

Never mind just how far we've veered from the circle of cool.

The kind of things I noticed almost immediately.

It took me only a few days in this school to realize a startling truth: everything I once thought I knew is no longer true.

For instance, I used to be so proud of the "Most Likely to Succeed" certificate I was awarded at the end of fifth grade, I even tacked it to my bedroom wall as a daily reminder of just how high my personal bar had been set.

But here at Greentree, all that certificate really means is that out of a class of thirty-five fifth graders, I'd been pegged as the one with the best shot of achieving social obscurity.

When it comes to seventh-grade girls, that certificate makes me only slightly more appealing than a bowlful of maggots.

Which is not to say that I'm repulsive to look at. 'Cause I'm not.

In the looks department, on a scale from Dougall Clement's crazy Einstein hair, vitamin D–deprived skin, and skinny body of the type some people call wiry to Josh Frost's obvious perfection, I'd say I'm closer to Josh.

I mean, we both have the kind of straight brown hair that sometimes flops in our eyes. We both have eyes that aren't exactly green or brown, so people call them hazel. And as for the rest of our features, well, they're pretty much standard issue—it's just that Josh's are better situated. And even though I had a two-inch growth spurt last summer, it still leaves me four inches shorter than Josh's five feet nine. But my mom swears I'm still growing, so there's hope that I'll catch up.

In other words, the raw materials are all there. And while I'm fully aware that there's nothing outstanding about me, I think it's worth noting that there's nothing especially hideous about me either.

Not like it makes a difference.

Seventh-grade girls like guys who are cool.

What they don't like are guys who, during the first week of the new school year, shout "Yes!" when their science teacher ambushes them with a pop quiz. Fist pump included.

They also don't like it when that same guy, oblivious to his classmates' searing looks of disdain, not only finishes his quiz first, but gets the perfect score that inspires the teacher to grade on a curve, deeming Smart Guy the one to beat.

While it may have made me the undisputed star of sixth-grade science, it's a move I will never live down. In the eyes of my peers, I became the Brainiac Nerd they should all work to avoid.

Not long after that, I embarked on what I secretly call my Campaign for Cool. I started by replacing that fifth-grade certificate on my wall with a poster of Josh Frost.

It probably seems weird to have the same poster on my wall that most girls tape inside their lockers, but I'm in desperate need of a social mentor. And since Josh is only five years older and grew up in the same town, even went to this school (maybe even sat in *this seat*!), well, clearly there's no one better to guide me.

Don't get me wrong; it's not like I'm some cautionary tale in the making. I fully intend to maintain my grades so I can get into a good college and live up to the promise of that fifth-grade certificate.

But first I'd really like to get a girlfriend, preferably one named Tinsley Barnes, before the end of seventh grade. Unlike Dougall, who refuses to adapt to the rules of our new social environment.

"I don't know about you," I say, hoping to switch the conversation to a much cooler subject, "but I plan to take back the clock for a nice long Christmas break, as soon as *this* final bell rings." I lean back even farther, folding my hands behind my head just like Mac Turtledove. Then I glance over at Tinsley and Ivy, willing them to notice, but they're too busy laughing hysterically at whatever Mac is saying.

"And then what?" Dougall frowns, waving his hand before me so I'll focus on him. "Soon as we return, we're right back to it. Heck, look at Sparks. . . ." He nods toward the front of the room. "What's he, like, fifty—sixty? He's been chasing the bell his whole life. It never ends."

"Thirty-four," Plum Bailey pipes up, and Dougall shifts toward her as I fix my gaze on the clock, urging the big hand to speed up. "Sparks. He's thirty-four." Plum swivels all the way around in her seat until she's facing me.

Even though I refuse to actually look at her, it's safe to

assume that her bony white hands are nervously twisting the sleeves of her sweater as her annoying brown eyes gawp my face, hoping I'll be dumb enough to accidentally return the look so she can grin at me with a mouthful of braces.

Let me backtrack.

When I said there isn't a single girl in this entire school who's remotely impressed by my brain, I wasn't counting Plum.

In my defense, I don't really think of Plum as a girl. I mean, she's got all the usual girl parts. Not that I've checked or anything. But she does wear a lot of homemade dresses and skirts, so I think that's safe to assume. And even though we used to kind of be friends, when it comes to things like social status, Plum isn't the kind of girl anyone notices.

She's like Dougall in that she mostly values the kinds of things no one else in this school gives a flying flip about. Reading, extra-credit assignments, good grades, getting excused from PE—same kinds of things I used to care about (and still secretly do), only, unlike Plum, I'm no longer in the business of advertising that part of myself.

Not to mention that, also unlike Plum, I had the good sense to hide my own mom-made Christmas sweater at the bottom of my backpack. The second you're seen in that thing, you're pretty much dead on arrival.

I guess what I'm trying to say is this: the fact that Plum is impressed by my being a Brain only goes to prove that being a Brain isn't cool.

But Dougall is somehow immune to all that, which is

why he actually risks speaking to Plum without even bothering to lower his voice.

"How could you possibly know that?" He squints, as though Sparks's age is part of a much bigger conspiracy.

"He's married to my mom's friend's cousin Chantal. She's from France. That's where they got married. My mom's friend's cousin even went to their wedding in Paris, and she—"

"Wait," I interrupt. "Sparks is *married? To a French lady? Named Chantal?*" I shift my attention back to Sparks, trying to make sense of how this could possibly happen.

Sparks—with his skinny arms and shiny scalp—the unhealthy obsession with diagramming sentences—and expressions so exaggerated he looks elastic, like he might snap at any second.

He's married to a Parisian lady with a superhot name, and I can't even get Tinsley Barnes to acknowledge my existence?

Is life seriously that unfair?

"My mom's friend's cousin said Paris is just as romantic in person as it is in the movies." Plum sighs, her gaze never once veering from me, as though she's imagining me whisking her there in a heart-shaped hot-air balloon. "Someday I really hope to visit—"

The sound of her voice is broken by the much anticipated *driiiiiiiing* of the school bell, which is all it takes to whip us from a state of complete inertia into an absolute frenzy of bodies stampeding for the door.

I grab my backpack, swing it over my shoulder, and shove

off my chair, ready to join the masses, when I discover that the numbness from my butt has spread to my feet. My legs will no longer hold me, and I face-plant smack onto the dirty tiled floor.

"Oh my gosh!" Plum squeals.

"Nick—you okay?" Dougall asks.

I lift my head just in time to see Tinsley Barnes and Ivy Wilburn step right over me like I'm nothing more than a felled tree in their path. The two of them head out the door in hot pursuit of Mac Turtledove.[2]

---

[2] This is clearly the moment when I should've called it quits and crawled home.

2

11:56 A.M.—12:17 P.M.

LUNCHTIME PURGATORY

If you were to survey a group of average middle school students, asking them to name their favorite class, nine out of ten would reply "lunch break," even though it doesn't qualify as an actual class. But if you were to ask me, I wouldn't hesitate to say, "Science, closely followed by math." Mainly because those thirty minutes between English and algebra pretty much qualify as my own personal hell.

My mom likes to claim that no matter how bad a situation may seem, it could always be worse, and in most cases that's true. I mean, at least I have Dougall to sit with, and most days Plum too.[3] But while eating on the small square of

---

[3] If it were up to me, Plum wouldn't sit with us. This is entirely Dougall's fault.

grass outside the library will never be considered as pathetic as choking down a sandwich in the hallway outside the bathrooms like the lowliest kids at our school, the fact that I'm one step above that untouchable crowd doesn't really provide the level of comfort you'd think.

I had high hopes when I started at Greentree. I'd spent most of the summer watching a bunch of teen movies so I'd know what to expect, and I fully imagined myself at the center of the cafeteria action with Tinsley on one side and Ivy on the other, only to instead get rejected from every table I attempted to join. Even the ones that were mostly empty shunned me with shaking heads and rolling eyes. Leaving me to wonder what my peers could possibly find so repulsive about me that they'd discard me on sight.

Maybe I didn't have the sort of automatic cool-table access granted to people like Tinsley, Ivy, and Mac Turtledove, who'd ruled from the top of the popularity pyramid stretching back to nursery school, but I was wearing new clothes, my hair looked more or less decent, and it's not like I smelled bad. But when Plum piped up from behind me, suggesting we all head outside, and when Dougall agreed, well, it suddenly became all too clear that my friends were the problem, not me.

Dougall and Plum might have been okay back in elementary school, but now that we were moving up in the world, there was no denying the fact that, between their weird clothes and even weirder interests, like Plum's love of reading just for the fun of it and Dougall's numerous conspiracy theories, they were keeping me from the elite life that should've been mine. As long as I continued to stay friends with them, my dreams of popularity would never be realized.

If you think that sounds cruel, then let me remind you that cafeteria politics are a harsh and merciless game. Every table is like a brutal medieval kingdom with a single blood-thirsty ruler at the helm, deciding on a whim who's in and who's out. Even the most minor infraction can result in banishment to a lesser table with no hope of return. In case you think that makes for an opening that needs to be filled, think again. In the one and a half years I've been at this school, I've never once seen someone ascend. But soon that will change, and the throne will be mine.

Until then, I'm left with no choice but to head to my own personal Siberia, which, like the cruel joke it is, requires me to walk right past the cool table.

Usually I duck my head and walk really fast, but today I do the unthinkable: I purposely stop right where Mac Turtle-dove sits. And even though my heart is beating like crazy and my armpits are all damp and sweaty, I still screw up the courage to look right at him and say, "Enjoy it while it lasts, Turtledove. Won't be long before you're eating in purgatory."

Okay, maybe I didn't actually say the words out loud.

Maybe I only said them in my head.

Still, just knowing it's true is a victory all its own.

Only, instead of moving on as I should, I continue to stand there like the nerd they're convinced that I am. Mainly because they all just continue talking and laughing like I'm completely invisible. Which, as far as superpowers go, would be a pretty cool one to have. But even the Invisible Man is seen some of the time. As far as these people are concerned, I don't even exist.

It's only when Dougall comes up behind me and says, "Nick, what the heck?" that I make for the other side of the room, push through the door, and head for the brown and balding butt-shaped patch of grass marking the space where every former Greentree failure has sat through the years.[4] And I can't help but wonder how Dougall will feel when we return from winter break and he's sitting here alone or, even worse, stuck with just Plum, since there's no way I can invite him to sit at the cool table with me. It makes me feel bad, since we're so used to eating together, but despite how powerful I'm about to become, there's no way I can bring him along if he refuses to change. Let's face it, for Dougall to be accepted by the people I'm about to become friends with, he'd have to transform pretty much everything about himself—the clothes, the personality—he'd basically have to become a completely different person.

"What took you so long?" Plum balances a cupcake with pink icing on the palm of her hand as her gaze settles on me. "Everything okay?"

I close my eyes and tilt my face toward the clouds, intent

_____
[4] On snow days we eat in the library. As long as we clean up our crumbs and don't spill, the librarians don't mind.

on ignoring her, which seems like the best way to go, even though it practically never works. No matter what I do, she insists on liking me in a way I will never reciprocate.

"Nick was having a staring contest with the back of Mac Turtledove's head." Dougall jabs a thumb at me and rolls his eyes.

"You have nothing to worry about." Plum's voice is so sincere it annoys me even more. "Mac doesn't stand a chance against you."

Dougall grunts, then flips the tab on the Coke he brought from home. And when I see the way it bubbles and spurts out the top, dribbling all over his hands, well, it's just one more example of why I have no choice but to lose him. There's no getting around it—Dougall is completely uncool.

"I still don't get why you're determined to do this." He wipes his hands on his jeans, seemingly unfazed by the fact that they're going to be sticky for the rest of the day.

"Nick has a gift." Plum shrugs like it's a fact. "And when you have a gift, you need to share it with the world."

"Please." Dougall tips his head back and laughs. "Nick's just trying to get Tinsley Barnes's attention."

I frown. There's no point in explaining myself when it's clear we have different ambitions, different visions. When I think about it, it's amazing our friendship has lasted this long.

"All I know is, Nick's going to crush it." Plum bites into her cupcake. "There's no doubt." She chases the words with a grin so big I'm practically blinded by the sight of chapped lips and small chunks of partially chewed cupcake stuck in her braces.

It's all the right words spoken by the exact wrong person. If that kind of support came from anyone else, like, seriously, *anyone* else, it might hold some meaning. Maybe even help boost my confidence. But coming from Plum, well, it just makes me desperate to leave. It may be the last day we'll all eat together, but I see no point in prolonging the inevitable.

I chuck my half-eaten sandwich back in my bag and stand.

"Where you going?" Dougall squints. "Bell hasn't even rung yet."

Again with the bells.

"I need a little prep time," I say, stealing the line Josh Frost always uses when he slips away for a few moments of silence before a big show.

Plum nods like she totally gets me, while Dougall screws up his face like he doesn't even know who I am.

And that's how I leave them—one nodding, one squinting—as I head back inside. And the funny thing is, I'm not even tempted to look back and wave goodbye.

12:48 P.M.—1:49 P.M.

GOOD OMEN #1[5]

In honor of Greentree's most famous (and only) homegrown celebrity, the gym received a makeover. There are blue and yellow streamers (our school colors) hanging from the ceiling and big yellow stars and WELCOME banners posted all over the walls. When Josh Frost takes the stage, well, even the most die-hard, self-proclaimed haters can't keep from getting caught up in the excitement of being in the same room as a real live, flesh-and-blood celebrity.

Everyone is shouting, clapping, and stomping their feet, and the girls are all screaming, "Josh—omigod, I love you!"

I'm too busy studying Josh to join the hysteria. The way

---

[5] Don't believe in good omens—they're not what they seem.

he stands before the mike, arms hanging casually by his sides, chin tilted ever so slightly, gaze moving slowly along the bleachers as though he's actually looking at each and every individual . . . well, it's clear why he rocketed straight to the top. For someone so used to screaming fans, he still manages to appear as though he's surprised by the attention.

The guy's a pro.

I can really learn a lot from him.

When the crowd starts clamoring for him to sing his new Christmas single, "Twelve Days," Josh just laughs and says the show's about *us*, not him. Which only makes the screams grow louder.

I breathe a sigh of relief. "Twelve Days" is the song I've been rehearsing, and Josh is such a superstar, I can't risk being overshadowed by him.

While he's busy charming the crowd with funny stories about his time here at Greentree, the teachers gather the performers backstage and make us line up in order of appearance.

Chloe Fields, a B-list seventh grader (she eats lunch at the second-coolest table), goes first. When she finally takes the stage and starts belting out a song, I'm shocked by how many people start clapping and singing along, because her voice isn't that great and it's clearly off-key. But no one seems to notice. They just act like they're enjoying it.

I shake my head, amazed at how low the bar is already set. Still, no matter how much they pretend to like it now, by the end of the show, Chloe Fields will be no more than a blur.

There's a strategy for everything in life, and talent shows are no different. If you have any hope of winning, you're better off going near the end. It guarantees a lasting impression.

I'm up second to last.

I consider it Good Omen #1.

Five sixth-grade guys go next, doing a pretty poor rendition of a boy-band song, if you ask me, but once again, other than a few boos quickly shut down by the school administrators, everyone gets into it.

Which only goes to show how boring Greentree can be.

We're so desperate for entertainment we'll clap for any lame act they stick in front of us.

"Nick, you sure about this?" Dougall, having snuck around the back, yanks on my hoodie, his expression clearly revealing what he's really thinking: *You're about to make an epic mistake by taking that stage—you're not nearly as gifted as you think.* Truth is, Dougall's never really supported my dreams, and he definitely doesn't get the importance of fully imagining the life you want to live. Not to mention, he's not a Josh Frost fan. When I put it all together, it's amazing we still get along. "We could bail right now. No one will even notice."

He says that like it's a good thing. Like it's not exactly why I need to do this. I'm tired of being so invisible that Tinsley and Ivy failed to notice me even when I fell right in front of them. I mean, I'm so easily ignored I didn't even have a chance to feel stupid. Hard to make a fool of yourself when nobody knows you exist.

"We could go to my house. Watch a Roswell documentary." His face animates at the thought of an afternoon spent on his couch, filling up on conspiracy theories and party-size bags of Cheetos. But I'm committed to seeing this through, and I'm sorry if Dougall doesn't agree. "Fine," he calls when I shake my head and move on. "Have it your way. You know where to find me."

Dougall may mean well, but his doubts are bringing me down when I need to stay positive. Besides, I'm saving my voice for the performance. The less I talk, the better. Which is exactly the excuse I use when Plum appears out of nowhere, or maybe she's been there all along—hard to tell when I'm so bent on ignoring her.

"Good luck, Nick!" She flashes a grin so big and hopeful I can't help but cringe.

I mean, sheesh. First Dougall bets against me, then Plum acts like some overeager groupie. Somewhere in this crowd lies a whole new set of much cooler friends.

"You got this!" she says, her fingers unexpectedly circling my wrist in a move so startling, I accidentally look right at her face just in time to see her eyes glint in a way that, for a split second, has me thinking she's halfway decent looking.

But before I lose it completely, I scowl and move away.

I'm beginning to regret that I was ever dumb enough to be nice to her. I mean, just because we used to be friends back in elementary school, when I didn't know any better, doesn't mean I don't know better now. Besides, now is not the time to encourage her. Not when my life is about to take flight.

I break away from the line of performers and slowly inch

toward the side of the stage where Josh Frost and some older guy with slicked-back hair and giant beefy Popeye arms who I recognize as his manager, Ben Ezer (only on Josh's show everyone just calls him Ezer), sit at a table with thick pads of paper, freshly sharpened pencils, and unopened bottles of water splayed out before them.

Ezer moves his pencil furiously across a page, but even after I tip on my toes and peer at his paper, I still can't decide if he's actually taking notes or is just bored and doodling.

Josh doesn't write anything. He keeps his focus on the performers, as though he's actually enjoying the slaughter of a Top 20 song.

When the music ends, our principal, Mrs. Partridge, introduces the next act. Ezer leans toward Josh and, speaking out of the side of his mouth, says, "Which band were they impersonating?"

I admit, the comment totally cracks me up. Especially when you consider how much effort went into Ian White's hair swoop, modeled after the lead singer's.

But then, when Ezer checks his watch and rolls his eyes, it's clear he's already tired, bored, and not taking this nearly as seriously as he should. Just seeing that makes my mood take a turn.

Whenever I'm upset, the first place it shows is my face. My dad used to joke that I should never play poker. Which I didn't exactly understand until Dougall explained that poker is a game best played by accomplished liars. Which is why his uncle lost everything—his money, his house, his wife, and his family. Apparently he was just like me—he wore the truth right smack in the middle of his face—and yet he still tried to get in on the game.

Anyway, the point is, that unhappy expression is exactly the one I'm wearing when Josh looks over his shoulder and sees me standing behind him.

"When are you up?" he asks, his voice rising like he's trying to lift my mood through sheer tenor alone.

"Second to last." I'm forced to choke out the words. I mean, I'm actually having a conversation with *Josh Frost*!

"Good luck!" He grins, turning away and nudging Ezer hard with his knee when Ezer pulls out his phone and starts checking his messages.

Before I can even think of a reply, Mrs. Partridge is tapping my shoulder and giving me her scary face as she points to where the performers are waiting and tells me to get back in line.

After a bunch of my classmates completely slaughter some of my favorite songs (including a performance by Mac Turtledove that receives way more applause than it deserves), it's my turn, and I can hardly believe that not one of the competitors thought to sing a Josh Frost song.

Probably weren't up for the challenge—afraid of humiliating themselves in front of an International Superstar.

I take it as Good Omen #2.[6]

I make for the stage, buzzing with the anticipation of a

---

[6] I really hope I don't have to remind you about good omens.

life that is about to irrevocably change in a very good way. Instead of being known as *The Brainiac Nerd Who Sucks at PE*, I'm moments away from being crowned *The Most Talented Kid at Greentree*.

I'm about to make Nerd History.

Thing is, the moment I'm standing before the mike, my palms go all clammy, my knees feel like they're about to disintegrate, and my throat and gut conspire on the most effective way to throw up.

My eyes dart back and forth, searching the crowd, frantically looking for someone who might actually be rooting for me. Dougall, Sparks, heck, I'm so desperate even Plum will do. But there are so many students and teachers the faces all smear together into a mass of people stomping and clapping, some hurling trash at the stage.

I can't do this.

There's no way.

This is not *at all* how I fully imagined it.

The noise grows louder as my 150 classmates huddle together, anticipating the moment I'll go down in flames.

I swipe my sweat-soaked palms down the front of my jeans and clear my throat repeatedly. I'm just about to claim laryngitis when I remember an early episode of *Frost World* where Josh talked about his first public performance and how he was sure he was going to hurl, until Ezer reminded him that people just want to be entertained and inspired and that it was Josh's job to go out and give it to 'em.

If it's good enough for Josh, it's good enough for me.

Besides, when I think about the performances we were all just subjected to, well, it's clear these people are in desperate need of a little inspiration.

I take a steady breath and lean toward the mike. "This one's for you," I say, pointing toward the general area where Tinsley Barnes usually sits in assemblies. I cue the music I rehearsed with the band yesterday after school, close my eyes for a moment, and pretend I'm singing to her.

At first my voice sounds kind of unstable, maybe even what you'd call croaky. But when I pick up the rhythm, everyone starts clapping, singing, and well, that's when I decide to go with the bigger of the two alternate endings I'd planned.

Ending #1 basically involves me bolting from the stage in case things go terribly wrong. It also includes an additional scene where I beg my parents to sell everything we own so we can move to a state far away, where nobody knows me.

But now, with everyone clearly enjoying the show, I go straight for Ending #2, which requires a perfectly executed *double-spin-hand-flash-wink-and-grin* before I take my final bow and say, "Be nice to everyone—let peace lead your way."

The official Josh Frost sign-off.

While it may sound simple in theory, the nearly simultaneous spinning, hand-flashing, winking, and grinning ends up making me so dizzy that by the time I lean in for the bow, my chin slams the top of the mike so hard it sends a loud *bfffffftt* sound screaming through the gym.

"Let peace be your guide," I mumble, knowing I've completely and totally blown it. Hardly able to believe I'd come so far, only to fall apart at the end.

The crowd was clearly mine. The plan I spent so much time fully imagining was a success! For the entire two minutes and forty-seven seconds I was singing, every single one of my classmates was clapping and singing right along with me.

Until I flubbed the sign-off and the clapping turned into laughing.

I turn away, practically racing from the stage, wanting more than anything to avoid looking at Josh, but I force myself anyway. The least I can do is apologize for trying to steal his signature move.

But when I look over to where he's sitting, the expression he wears is as unmistakable as a report card smothered with As.

Josh Frost is nodding.

Grinning.

Giving me an enthusiastic thumbs-up.

And I'm pretty dang sure he didn't do that for anyone else.

4

1:52 P.M.—2:16 P.M.

FROSTED

An eighth-grade drama die-hard takes the stage last in a blur of jazz hands and clumsy dance moves. But now that I know I've got Josh's vote, I don't bother watching.

In my head I can still hear the crowd clapping and singing, can still see the approval on Josh's face. The arc of his thumb as he jabbed it toward me, as if to silently say, *You got this!*

And to think it's just the beginning.

Won't be long before that kind of praise becomes a regular thing.

When the music ends, our class president hogs the mike and drones on and on about all of the supposedly exciting things happening at Greentree after winter break and blah, blah, blah.

I mean, is she serious? Can't she see there's not a single person here (other than her) who gives a flying flip about any of that?

The only thing these people are interested in is hearing the name of the winner so they know who to suck up to for the rest of the year.

The other performers gather behind me. All of them are busy high-fiving and complimenting each other's mediocre performances. But not me. I sneak away from the group and linger near the stage. Better to be close to the steps when they announce me as the winner.

Also, if I lean in just so, I can actually make out a lot of what Ezer and Josh Frost are saying.

I inch closer, straining to hear. Barely able to breathe when Josh says, "I'm liking that kid at the end."

Kid at the end?

A slow panic churns in my gut.

Does he mean the kid at the end-end? The high-kicking, jazz-handing drama nerd?

The one I ignored?

Is it possible the thumbs-up and eye-smile didn't mean what I thought?

"That last one?" Ezer's expression betrays just how he feels about that. "You're joking."

"No. The one who went right before him." Josh reaches

for his water and twists the cap back and forth as though he's actually nervous about stating his opinion to Ezer, even though everyone knows Ezer works for him.

"Ah. 'Twelve Days.'" Ezer's voice is impossible to read.

"That's it. He's the one." Josh takes a long, steady drink as I use all of my strength to force my grin into submission.

"I don't know." Ezer frowns. "He's a little rough around the edges. And the way he copied your signature move—didn't that strike you as overly ingratiating?"

"Like you can ever be overly ingratiating in this business?" Josh laughs at a joke I'm not sure I get. Shaking his head, he adds, "He reminds me of myself when I was his age. I was rough too. Besides, that kind of awkwardness and adulation always makes for good TV."

That's it. That's all I needed to hear.

Who cares if Josh called me awkward—I'm in!

In just a matter of seconds it'll be goodbye, Brainiac Nerd—hello, International Superstar!

Dreams really do come true.

I'm living proof.

I make my way toward the rest of the performers and high-five with the rest of them, even lob a few fake compliments of my own, all the while feeling sorry that they don't stand a chance.

There can be only one winner.

And it just so happens it's me.

I gush over Chloe Fields's total fail of a song.

I even say something nice to Ian White about his hair swoop.

It's just like Josh always says: *Be nice to everyone—let peace lead your way.*

I glance toward the stage, inwardly rehearsing a few fake surprised expressions when Josh starts by congratulating everyone on a job well done ... how Greentree is bursting with talent ... and on and on to the point where I really wish he'd just announce me already so I can start my new life.

Still, despite my excitement, I remind myself to stay humble and cool. To wait for my full name to be called before I react.

And yet, the second Josh says, "And the winner of the Greentree Talent Show is—" I leap right past my fake surprised look and bolt for the stage wearing a grin so big, my face feels like it's cleaved right in half.

My right foot is just about to meet the first step when Mac Turtledove shoves past me so hard I lose my balance, my knees crumble, and I land smack on the edge.

"Move it, loser," Mac barks, leaving me clutching both knees in pain and watching through unbelieving eyes as he claims his place beside Josh.[7]

The sight of them standing together is all it takes to get the crowd on their feet, clapping and screaming like crazy, as the opening strains of Josh's new hit single, "Twelve Days," blares through the gym.

[7] I really hate Mac Turtledove.

"Why don't you help me out here in case I forget the lyrics!" Josh laughs, tossing an arm around Mac's shoulders as though they're old friends.

And when the two of them start singing, it sounds as though they've been rehearsing for weeks. Except for the part where Mac flubs a few lyrics and everyone pretends not to notice.

It's a hideous sight, but I can't seem to stop watching, much less convince myself to get up and get the heck out before it gets any worse.

While Josh and Mac charm the crowd, Ezer collects his belongings like the gym is on fire and he's desperate to flee, so I hobble over to where he stands, clear my throat, and say, "There's been a mistake." Kind of semi-shouting so he'll hear me over the music, but he completely ignores me.

Despite the shooting pain in my legs, despite a gut that feels like it's waging a serious protest against everything I ate over the course of the last several weeks, I move closer, desperate to fix this before it's too late.

"Excuse me," I say. "But there's been a—"

"No mistake, kid." He barks the words over his shoulder like he can't be bothered to actually face me.

"But I think there was," I insist. "No, I mean, I'm *sure* there was. That was supposed to be *me* up there. I'm one hundred and ten percent sure of it."

That got him to look, his hard, squinty gaze floating over my face as he says, "Oh yeah? And what makes you think that?"

"I was standing right here when I heard Josh vote for the kid near the end who sang 'Twelve Days.' That kid was me. I'm that kid."

Ezer grunts and closes his eyes in the same way my mom does when she's striving for patience and inwardly counting to ten. "Turns out I have the power to veto, so I did." He turns away, as though the argument's over.

"But—" I glare at the back of his neck, like a tree stump holding up an enormous head. My voice sounds pathetic and wimpy, but still, I push the words past. "The rules *clearly* state that *Josh* is supposed to choose the winner. Josh Frost. *Not* you!" For whatever reason, that makes him laugh.

"Listen, kid." Ezer glances between the stage and me. "You know that indefinable thing that makes someone a star—someone worth watching?"

I stare at him, barely able to breathe.

"You ain't got it."

The words are like an arrow to my heart.

Yet I still manage to protest. "And Mac Turtledove does?" I know it sounds childish. It sounds even worse in person.

But when Ezer points to the stage, where Josh and Mac are well into the finale, I hate to admit it, but there's no denying he's right.

There's a reason Mac Turtledove's name is enshrined in a heart on nearly every girl's notebook.

He has *it*.

That indefinable thing that makes people want to watch him.

Be near him.

Worship him from afar.

"Everyone wants to be a star," Ezer says. "For most, it's just a big waste of time. Do yourself a favor and find another dream—something a little more reasonable. May hurt to hear it now, but trust me, someday you'll look back and thank me. Nothing wrong with knowing your limits."[8]

The song ends.

Josh and Mac exit the stage.

And my new life is officially over before it could begin.

[8] This is the exact opposite of what Josh Frost says. He's always encouraging us fans to go after our dreams, but now I'm wondering if he really means it.

5

2:32 P.M.—2:41 P.M.

SUGARPLUM FAIRY

I'm halfway home when I hear it—the all-too-familiar gasping, wheezing sound of Plum Bailey's voice.

"Nick!" She races to catch up, panting so loudly I can no longer pretend not to hear. "I can't believe you didn't win! You were, like, a million times better than that phony Mac Turtledove!"

Before I can stop myself, I laugh. I mean, it's not like I want to encourage her. I guess I'm just so used to girls slobbering all over Turtledove, it's shocking to hear one of them call him a phony.

"Seriously," she says, going on and on about Mac being a big wannabe who gave a bogus performance as I glare at the long stretch of sidewalk unspooling before me that, in reality, isn't actually all that long, but with Plum so determined to stalk me, well, it feels like it goes on forever.

She probably thinks that by trashing Mac, she'll make me feel better, but the truth is, pointing out how I lost to a poseur just makes it worse.

I hit the bend in the walk that leads to my drive, escape finally within reach, when she tugs hard on my sleeve. "Don't you think you should change?" She uncurls a bony finger to point at my Greentree hoodie, but I have no idea what she's talking about. "The Christmas sweater. The one your mom made you wear. I saw you shove it into your backpack just before school. You should put it back on before she sees."

She says it so openly. Like she's not the least bit embarrassed to admit she was watching me without my consent.

Still, there's no doubt she's right. My mom would be really hurt if she ever found out I was so embarrassed by the sweater she knit, I hid it in my backpack. [9]

For once, Plum's obsession with me did me some good.

I yank the sweater over my hoodie, which makes it look a little bulky and strange, but I'm in a hurry to get away from Plum, and my mom will be so happy to see me wearing it, she won't even notice the lumps. As soon as the sweater's in place and I'm more or less situated, I try to leave again, but Plum steps before me, wearing this weird expression

---

[9] Mom, if you're reading this, I'm sorry I had to include this part. I was only trying to give an honest account of how I felt *then*. Clearly I don't feel that way now. Please keep that in mind as you continue to read. Also, I'm sorry that because of my decision to accept a ride from a crazy person, the sweater you knit will end up spending the rest of eternity in an evidence locker.

(weirder than usual), and then she shoves a red-and-green box into my chest.

"Happy birthday!" she cries, her face turning so red I'm tempted to run away and never look back.

"Today's not my birthday," I tell her, trying to keep from frowning as I push the box away. I don't want to be rude, but there's no way I'm accepting that. It's like the final insult on a complete failure of a day.

Had things gone as I'd fully imagined, Tinsley would be standing here instead.

But Plum refuses to take it, even going so far as to bend my fingers around it. "Your birthday's on Christmas, I know." She smiles brightly, too brightly, as though she refuses to acknowledge how desperate I am to be rid of her. "I just thought I should give it to you now." She tucks a chunk of blond hair, the color of a bowl of soggy Cheerios, behind her ears, but the curls won't be tamed and spring right back again. "I know how sometimes your birthday gets over-shadowed by all the holiday stuff, and I wanted you to know I didn't forget." Her voice is shaky, her face wild and flushed. It's the same look I've seen during the backstage meet and greets on the Josh Frost show. The look every girl who goes before him gets when she imagines the day they'll be married with little Frost babies of their own and time can't move quickly enough.

I turn away, eager to put this whole mess behind me. But of course she insists on following me all the way to the top of my drive. "I made it especially for you," she says, as though it adds some kind of value, when the truth is, I'm not the least bit curious as to what waits inside. "You don't have to open it now, of course. But don't wait too long. It won't last forever."

"Got it," I say, hoping this is it and she'll finally move on. I mean, how much longer does she plan on beating this horse?

"I even made the candle."

I close my eyes, imagining myself as the stallion she insists on whipping long past the moment I've heaved my last breath.

"It was really fun to make. Oh, and there's a small box of matches too, so don't forget to make a wish. And make sure it's a good one. There's power in a wish—don't waste it on the mundane."

I frown in a way that takes over my face and make no attempt to hide it.

If wishes came true, I wouldn't be standing here now.

I'd be in a limo with Josh on one side and Tinsley on the other, speeding down the highway toward fortune and fame.

Plum's lips start to spasm as her eyes go all squinty and tight. But even though I'm sure it's my fault, I'm already feeling crummy enough. I don't have room for Plum's crummy stuff too.

"Hope you have a good birthday," she calls as I race for my door, desperate to be rid of her. "And remember, choose your wish carefully—sometimes they really do come true!"

6

2:43 P.M.—4:41 P.M.

TINSEL MADNESS

After ditching Plum's gift on the kitchen counter, I head upstairs to my room, where I immediately get started on the
First Order of Business, which is to rip the Josh Frost poster
from my wall and shred it into tiny, unrecognizable bits.

Not that I actually blame Josh.

Or at least not entirely.

While it's nice to know he saw my potential, it clearly
wasn't enough to get him to override Ezer. And as much as
I once admired him, turns out Josh isn't the hero I thought.

He let me down.

And now it's time to move on.

"What's all this?" My older sister barges into my space.
She doesn't even bother to knock, despite the sign on my

door with these clearly stated instructions. "Oh no—did you and Josh break up?"

I glare at the space on my wall where the tape that once held the poster has removed four rectangles of eggshell-colored paint and wait for her to leave.

"Does it have anything to do with that sweater you're wearing?" She laughs way too hard at her own dumb joke. She always thinks she's funnier than she is. "Please tell me you didn't actually wear that to school." Her voice is kind of loud, like she doesn't even care if our mom overhears.[10]

"Get out of my room, Holly." I keep my back turned. No point in looking when the image of her long dark hair, smirky face, and dumb ironic T-shirt is practically tattooed on my brain.

"I'm not *in* your room," she says, which means she's hovering just shy of the doorway. The usual game.

"Get out of my proximity, then," I say. My usual reply.

"Happily. But not until I fulfill my sisterly duty and tell you that Mom needs your help hanging the garland and wreaths and whatever else she needs to get ready for the tree. Dad's bringing it home tonight. You're supposed to help with that too."

Inwardly I groan. I'm not really feeling the holiday spirit. I mean, why does it always have to be me? Why can't Holly do something for a change?

---

[10] Mom and Dad, if you're reading this, then maybe you'll finally see what I've been telling you all along: Holly is not a nice person. This is just one example of what I've been forced to put up with for the last almost-thirteen years.

I'm about to ask exactly that when she says, "Not only am I older than you, but I'm also smarter than you, which means I figured out long ago how to *recuse* myself from Mom's annual bout of Christmas craziness. This one's on you, Nick."

Typical Holly. Using a word like *recuse* and pronouncing it in a big-deal way to show off her fancy vocabulary.

I turn, wanting her to see my eyes purposely rolling. And that's when I confirm that her hair really is hanging in her face, her expression is the dictionary definition of smirky, and today's T-shirt reads DEAR SANTA, THE NAUGHTY LIST STARTS HERE, with an arrow pointing up toward her chin.

"Nice." I roll my eyes again, watching Holly bob her knees into a fake curtsy.

Even though my mom is pretty much annoy-proof during the holidays, even though she's used to Holly's politics and protests, she still has her limits. Which is why I've been tapped as her go-to child from December 19 to January 2.

Everyone's mom has a thing. Plum's mom is really into cooking and knitting. Dougall's is really into her new family to the point where she often forgets about Dougall. And my mom practically lives for Christmas. I mean, who else names their kids Nick and Holly? Also, she loves to tell the story of how she convinced her doctor to induce my delivery a few days early so I'd be born on Christmas Day—like she expects me to thank her or something.

Back when I was little and didn't know any better, I thought it was cool to be born on Christmas. I actually believed that the lights and decorations and trees all over the neighborhood were put there to celebrate *me*.

By the time I hit kindergarten, I'd learned the harsh truth. And the thing is, it's just like Plum says—when your birthday falls on Christmas, it tends to get overshadowed by a much *bigger* birthday.

Still, just because Holly has trained my mom into thinking she's unable to help out during the holidays, that doesn't mean I'm willing to play along. I've come to dread this time of year for much better reasons than hers.

"Come on, Holly," I say. "Why can't you do something nice for a change and help Mom instead?" My voice sounds a little whinier than I'd like, but really, I'm so desperate it's not like I care.

"Because she specifically asked for you." Holly has an answer for everything. "Besides, you know I don't participate in manufactured Hallmark holidays."

"Christmas is a Hallmark holiday?" I roll my eyes a third time. It's become the only expression I'm capable of around her.

"It is now." Her mouth twists to one side as her eyebrows do that thing where they shoot halfway up her forehead. "It's all about shopping and spending—it's mass consumerism at its worst."

"And yet, you still have no problem cashing Nana's annual Christmas check."

"Only so I can donate half the proceeds to Unicef." She

turns away, as though I'll actually let that one slide. As if I don't know better. Holly is quite possibly the most selfish person I've ever met.

"And the other half? What'd you do with that? Is that how you bought the charming T-shirt you're wearing?"

Holly glares and heads down the hall, her voice trailing off as she says, "Like I said, Mom wants you downstairs."

★

"Nick—there you are—just in time!"

My mom tips her head in a way that causes her to teeter even more precariously from the top of the stepladder. With a length of garland gripped between her teeth and a Christmas wreath looped around her neck, she looks like she's putting on some kind of bizarre Yuletide performance.

"Can you help me out here? Just hold the ladder steady and let me know if the garland swoops are equally spaced."

She hitches onto her toes and reaches toward the ceiling in a way that makes me fear for her safety, but when it comes to decorating for Christmas, my mom's all too willing to test the theory of gravity.

Other than a few minor edits, it's pretty much the same decor every year. And while I guess it looks nice enough, I've never understood her insistence on the fake snow and icicles when there's usually no shortage of the real thing right outside the front door.

"How was school?" she asks, the words muffled by the

tack she's now placed between her front teeth, sharp side in. Another dangerous move, but to my mom, it's all about the craft.

"Terrible," I say, mostly to see if she's really listening.

"That Josh Frost was there today, wasn't he?" she asks, proving she's not really listening, just making small talk. Her voice brightens when she adds, "How'd that go?"

"Awful." I free up a length of garland, watching as one of her feet completely loses contact with the ladder as she stretches along the wall, veering way past my comfort zone.

"That must've been exciting for you." She rights herself again and climbs back down to survey her work, pulling at the sleeves of a Christmas sweater that's more embarrassing than mine, then pushing a hand through a cloud of shortish dark hair that's best described as practical.

"Mmmm" is the best I can manage. No point in saying anything more when, yet again, we've come to that most wonderful time of the year, when I, Nick Dashaway, my mother's very own Christmas miracle, am rendered invisible.

I glance around the room, taking in the three red felt stockings hung by the chimney with care, including one for our dog, Sir Dasher Dashaway[11]; the jars crammed full of chocolates and candy canes; the tinsel draped over just about every surface that's not covered with a garland, a poinsettia, or an icicle; all the way to the enormous plastic bins stuffed

---

[11] In defense of his name, Holly and I were very young when we got him, and we thought it sounded distinguished.

full of ornaments, all lined up and ready to go, just waiting for the tree to arrive.

Oh, and did I mention the continuous loop of Christmas carols that plays in the background? It's pretty much the Dashaway sound track until January 2.

Tinsel Madness. That's what this is.

Everything in my life leans to the extreme.

My sister is *extremely* annoying.

My mom is *extremely* Christmas obsessed.

My dad is *extremely* stressed over his business ever since The Depot opened in the town next to ours.

My dog has an *extremely* bad case of flatulence.

My friends are *extremely* nerdy.

And the *extremely* cool life that I dreamed of is *extremely* over before it could actually get off the ground.

"So, what do you think?" My mom looks between her holiday masterpiece-in-the-making and me.

"Looks like you've done it again," I say, not wanting to hurt her feelings. When I see the way she grins in response, I feel better for trying. Just because *my* day sucked doesn't mean I need to take hostages and make everyone else miserable too.

While my mom fusses with decorations that don't require the use of a stepladder, I eat a microwaved dinner alone at the counter. The table is reserved for decorating the hundreds of cookies the oven will begin regurgitating on a regular basis within the next hour so my mom can package them as gifts for neighbors, the postman, and pretty much everyone we know, including people we barely know. Then I grab the microwaved meal my mom packed for my dad and head out for the first night of my unofficial (and officially unpaid) holiday job at the Dashaway Home and Hardware.

Even though I sometimes complain about not getting paid, for the most part I really don't mind. I've been hanging around the shop since I was a kid, though it wasn't until last summer that my dad gave me an actual schedule and taught me how to run the cash register. My dad's a good guy, and I like spending time with him when he's not totally stressed, which these days is practically never. Then again, it's always kind of hectic around the holidays. Christmas is the busiest time of year on account of the Christmas tree lot my dad runs in the back, so it's good that I'll be there to help if he needs me.

The usual routine goes like this: I ride my bike to the shop, showing up more or less on time, then I hand over the food and cover the register while my dad eats in his office. Then, when it's time to close up shop, we toss my bike in the back of his truck and he drives us both home. It's an okay arrangement, I guess, but this year I'm hoping we can change it up a bit.

For the longest time I've been begging to help out on the Christmas tree lot, which is so much cooler than ringing up lightbulbs and toilet plungers for the parents of the class-mates who refuse to acknowledge me.

The lot is where the action is. But until now, my dad said I was too short and scrawny to be of much help.[12] So instead he always hires one or two kids from the local high school.

But my growth spurt last summer also resulted in seven additional pounds, some of which is genuine muscle. Not to mention the two inches tacked on to my height. And if my dad's been too stressed to notice, then I guess I'll just have to show him.

[12] Okay, so maybe he didn't say those actual words, but trust me, it was implied.

7

5:25 P.M.—7:45 P.M.

THREE TURTLEDOVES

"Hey, kiddo," my dad calls the second I walk through the door.

I pause. Telling myself, not for the first time, that I really need to ask him to stop calling me that. I'm older now. The nickname no longer fits.

Problem is, right before he saw me, I saw him. And with his hair all gray and his face all creased, well, he looked so tired I can't bring myself to do it. So I head into his office and deposit his dinner on his desk before joining him in the aisle where all the sealants and glues are displayed.

"How was school?" he asks, and I'm just about to answer when Sir Dasher Dashaway, the store's unofficial mascot, runs over to greet me, farting the entire way.

"Aw, Dash." I plug my nose with one hand and pet him with the other.

"He's getting old." My dad reaches for a can of holiday-themed air freshener, practically nuking the place with a cinnamon-and-clove-scented cloud.

"Is that what's gonna happen to you?" I joke, just as two cars pull up to the front of the store, headlights blazing so brightly through the window that we're temporarily blinded.

"Think they're here for a new sprinkler system?" my dad asks. Though, unfortunately for him, his poker face is as bad as mine, and well before he can get the words out, he's already grinning.

It's a game we play. We try to guess what a customer will ask for by picking one of the store's more obscure or off-season offerings, only to see if we're right.

One time I guessed a stack of beach towels in the middle of a snowstorm, and dang if Plum's mom didn't come in on her way to her sister's house in Florida, looking for precisely that.

The win earned me a crumpled ten-dollar bill plucked fresh from the register, which I put toward the latest Josh Frost CD. But this time, before I can guess, the engines cut, the lights dim, and the Turtledove family, including Mac, springs into view.

Mr. Turtledove climbs out of his customized truck, pushing through the door with a hearty "Hello!," while Mrs. Turtledove and her lovely son, Mac, continue to sit in her big fat Mercedes, cell phones glued to their ears.

They're probably fielding calls from Hollywood agents who heard about the latest Greentree sensation.

"Better make it quick," my dad whispers, still waiting for my guess.

I just shrug. Seeing Mac Turtledove has wiped the fun out of me.

My dad shoots me a look of concern, but a moment later he's crossing the room to shake hands with Mr. Turtledove, who, believe it or not, he knew back in high school.

That's the thing about Greentree. Most of the people who live here were born here, and I guess they got too lazy to leave. It's definitely not the kind of place anyone would ever choose to move to, other than Dougall and his dad, but I guess they had their reasons.

Mr. Turtledove shoots me a quick nod and wave, but honestly, I doubt he even knows my name. He's the kind of guy who's big with the hellos and the meaningless chatter, but he never really remembers your face unless he's been looking at it for the last thirty-some years, like my dad's. Also, he's more of a seasonal shopper, coming in for pool umbrellas in the summer or fire logs in the winter. He'd hardly be considered a regular.

But tonight, according to him, he's here for a tree.

Let the festivities begin.

"Gotta tell ya, Dashaway"—he hitches his thumbs into his belt loops like he's some kind of rugged ranch hand instead of a real estate agent with his picture posted on notepads and bus stops all over this town—"I ventured over to

The Depot, just to check out their stock, only to discover their trees aren't nearly as impressive as yours. I gotta hand it to ya, Dashaway, you always seem to outdo yourself."

Aside from being a photogenic real estate agent, Mr. Turtledove is also a former jock who calls everyone by their last name.

"So how about you take me to the biggest tree on your lot, and you and I can work out a price?" He shoots my dad this enormous grin, all white teeth and gold fillings.

This again. I allow myself a smirk. Every year it's the same routine. Turtledove asks for the biggest tree on the lot, while my dad steers him to the second-biggest tree, thereby saving the biggest for our family.

It's one of the major benefits of running a Christmas tree lot.

I head for the office, figuring I'll do my dad a solid and get his dinner nuked so it'll be ready when he's finished dealing with Turtledove. I pull the microwave meal from the cooler pack and notice that my mom included Plum's gift when I wasn't looking, which must mean it's edible, not that I check.

Once the meal is in motion, the carousel circling slowly, I pass by the window, hoping to catch a glimpse of my dad duping Turtledove yet again, when Turtledove says, "And this year, I don't want your second-biggest tree. I want your *absolute biggest* tree." He smiles in a way that only his lips are participating. "Jig's up, Dashaway. I know you've been saving the best for yourself, but this year I'm paying top dollar. With the way things are going, now that The Depot's moved in, you might want to reconsider this little game of yours."

I smash my cheek against the cold glass, watching as my dad—without the slightest hesitation, without even putting up a fight—leads him straight to the tree we tagged as ours.

And it's only a few moments later when he's standing in the doorway, saying, "Come on, now's your big chance. I need some help loading up a tree, and it turns out you're just the man for the job." He tries to make it sound like a reason to celebrate, but one look at his face and it's easy to see just how much this is costing him.

"What about Steve, or Rick?" I say, refusing to budge from my place. "Or whatever high school kid you hired this year?"

My dad squints in a way that makes his hazel eyes—eyes that look just like mine—sort of recede. "Didn't hire anyone." He wipes a hand across his brow. "Figured you were the only man I needed." When that still doesn't convince me, he says, "Nick, what gives?" His voice betrays his irritation. "You've been begging for this job since you were five. Your wish came true. Now let's go—Turtledove's waiting!"

My wish came true.

Wrong wish, but hey, what's the difference?

I really want to stand my ground. Say no way José and point out the all-too-obvious fact that between my dad, King Turtledove, Prince Turtledove, and yeah, even Queen Turtledove, they should be able to handle it themselves. I mean, if they're so intent on stealing our tree (never mind that he's paying top dollar for it), then surely they can manage to heave it into His Majesty's customized truck.

But when the lines on my dad's forehead sink even deeper, there's really no choice but surrender.

I mean, what's one more humiliation in an otherwise completely humiliating day?

It's not until I'm already outside and see Mac leaning against his mom's Mercedes in that annoying movie-star way, phone still glued to his ear, that I remember I'm still wearing the extremely unfortunate homemade Christmas sweater.

The one featuring a giant reindeer with a bright red nose made of an actual pom-pom.

The second he sees it, Mac starts howling. Hand-clutching-belly, doubled-over howling. Stopping long enough to snap a cell-phone pic, probably so he can text it to all his cool-table friends, before he starts howling again.[13]

I duck my head and push past him. I mean, he's already seen it, so there's no use hiding. I follow my dad deep into the lot, and we practically kill ourselves hauling the monster tree into the bed of Turtledove's truck while His Highness stands on the sidelines, giving us repeated warnings to be mindful of his customized paint job.

When it's finally over, Mac is *still* going on about my sweater as he decides to ride home with his dad. Mrs. Turtledove, having eyeballed the horizontal tree from the comfort

---

[13] I really, really hate Mac Turtledove.

of her Mercedes, squints her approval and leaves. My dad and I are now stiff with sap, itching from pine needles, and staring into the Turtledoves' dust as the family caravans off the lot.

"So, what'd you think?" my dad says. "Was it everything you dreamed it would be? Biggest one on the lot. It can only get easier from here!" He grins and slaps a friendly hand on my back, going to great lengths to make the situation seem so much better than it is. But it's clear he's feeling as defeated as I do.

My first impulse is to say something crummy, but I don't have the heart. I'm tired of the Turtledoves. Tired of today. Tired of seeing my dad look so tired.

I smile weakly and follow him back inside the shop. His cell phone starts chiming, and my mom's voice blares through the speaker, asking how soon she can expect the tree to be delivered.

"Why don't you go hang out in the office?" My dad presses a hand over the speaker. "Clean yourself up. Take a load off."

"But what about your dinner?" I say, wanting to stick around, see how he'll break the news to my mom. "I put it in the microwave. It should be ready by now."

"I'll get to it." He winks, turning away and moving to the far side of the store, where I won't be able to eavesdrop so easily.

I head into the small bathroom and try to clean off, though there's not much I can do about the sap on my jeans;

59

it hardens like glue and makes the legs so stiff I walk like a robot. Then I sit in my dad's chair and spin in circles, which gets old pretty fast, so I call over Sir Dasher Dashaway and spend my time alternately petting him and clearing the air with peppermint-scented spray. And though my dad does his best to speak in hushed tones, every now and then I can hear him mumble things like "back taxes" and "year-end financials" in a voice thick with worry. It seems like every conversation they have reverts to those things.

When he's done talking to my mom, he steps into the office, looking even wearier than before. "Why don't you head on home, Nick?" he says. "You've done enough for your first night on the job. Save some of that energy for tomorrow. I need you here bright and early."

"But what about you?" I ask, refusing to budge. We always go home together. It's a tradition. We can't break it now.

"It's going to be a late one." He forces a smile. "You know, Christmas rush and all. Besides, your mother needs help finishing the decorations. If you leave now, you can still catch the bus. I'll get your bike home. Better hurry, though. Last bus leaves in fifteen minutes."

Against my better judgment, I grab my stuff and head out. When my dad gets that determined, there's no point arguing.

I've just reached the door when he calls me back. Thinking he changed his mind, I turn excitedly, only to find him standing behind me with Plum's gift in his hand.

I wave it away. "It's all yours," I tell him.

"No, it's definitely yours," he says. "There's a note inside with your name on it."

He shoots me this sort of twinkly look, which instantly makes me feel queasy. I mean, if the note was from Tinsley, I might be all twinkly-eyed too. But the fact that it's from Plum . . . well, I wish this stupid box would just disappear.

Of course I end up taking it. He's pretty much insisting. So I carry the dumb red-and-green box all the way to the bus stop, where I plop down on the seat, lean my back against a picture of Mr. Turtledove's smiling face promising to sell you the home of your dreams, and wait for this day to be over.

8

7:46 P.M.—8:16 P.M.

RUN, RUN, RUDOLPH

The first time my parents let me ride the bus by myself, I was ten years old and felt like I'd finally arrived.

Everything seemed better than it was. The seats were cleaner. The driver was friendlier. The fellow passengers were happier. And every window offered a view so spectacular I didn't want it to end.

That was nearly three years ago, and now I'm just hoping the bus will show up. Then I can get back to my room and barricade myself inside until winter break is over and my parents are forced to smash through the door and drag me back to school.

A blast of cold wind curls down the street, delivering a chill so intense I pull the hoodie I'm still wearing over my head. When it fails to provide the kind of insulation I need, I reach into my backpack for the hat, scarf, and mittens that match the sweater, red pom-poms included. Every year my mom makes a new set, presenting it with such excitement I don't have the heart to tell her the years of Plum, Dougall, and I coordinating our Christmas-themed sweaters are over. The only reason I'm wearing this now is sheer desperation.

I put the hat on under the hood, pulling it so low and the scarf so high that my eyes are the only things left uncovered. Any other day I'd seriously choose death by hypothermia over wearing one of my mom's Christmas creations.[14] But since I've pretty much reached the place known as Rock Bottom, I figure I have nothing to lose. If I'm doomed to be a Brainiac Nerd for the rest of my life, I might as well be a warm and toasty one.

I'm about ten minutes into the wait when I notice that not a single car has gone by, which strikes me as strange.

Not like I'm expecting a traffic jam. Greentree Avenue is hardly Times Square or Hollywood Boulevard. Still, even a small town like ours usually sees a little more action than this, especially on a Friday night.

After about twenty minutes I start to wonder if my dad got the schedule mixed up. I grab my cell, about to call my mom and ask her to come pick me up, only to discover that my phone has no service, which is really weird, since that's never happened in this area before and it's not like I'm in the middle of nowhere.

---

[14] Mom, please reread footnote #9.

This bus stop is smack in the center of the Greentree business district, which, while not nearly as impressive as it sounds—it's basically two short blocks stuffed with store-fronts and office buildings—is not exactly Siberia.

From what I can see, I've got three options:

#1: Head back to the store and wait it out until my dad's ready to leave.

It seems reasonable on the surface, but if I leave now, I'll risk missing the bus, which may show up at any minute.

Not to mention it will probably make my dad feel like he needs to leave the store early, which means he won't get his work done, which will only add to his stress level, which is high enough already.

#2: Suck it up, deal with the cold, and start walking home.

Only this option isn't nearly as reasonable as it seems, since it's seriously cold out, and even with the scarf, hat, and mittens, I'm pretty positive I'll keel over from frostbite well before I get home.

#3: Stay right where I am—hunkered down in the shelter of the bus stop with Mr. Turtledove's face grinning into my back.

After careful consideration, Option #3 is clearly the winner.

But as the snow starts to fall and actually sticks, I'm seriously starting to think this could very well be the end of me, when I remember Plum's gift—or, more important, the candle that's supposedly waiting inside.

I crack the box open, and sure enough, there's a birthday candle with red and green swirls running all along the sides and a small box of matches, just like she said.

Oh, and there's also a cupcake decorated with a giant gold star, like she was sure I was going to win the talent show.

Or maybe it means that whatever happens, I'm still a star in her eyes.

Whatever. It's not like I'm planning to eat it.

There's also the note my dad mentioned, but the second I read

Dear Nick, I hope that when you blow out this candle, your greatest wish will come true. . . .

I lose interest, toss it aside, shove the candle in the middle of the star, and strike a match on the side of the box, only to watch it instantly fizzle.

The ones that follow meet the same fate until I'm down to the very last match, which I cradle like a baby, making a shelter with my hands like I've seen my dad do when he's lighting a campfire. Not daring to so much as breathe, I hear the quick bursting sizzle of flame meeting wick. The tiny blaze glimmers for a handful of seconds before it settles into a small but adequate flame that warms the tips of my mitten-covered fingers.

I sit like that for a while. Probably looking like some demented Christmas clown, all huddled over a cupcake candle, having finally reached the ultimate level of dorkdom yet vowing to remain on this bench until the candle burns out—which shouldn't take long—and if the bus still hasn't come, I'll get my butt moving and risk hypothermia.

Fat globs of wax drool onto the icing, dotting the bright gold star with sludgy red and green circles that turn this ugly maroonish color the second they mix. The candle continues to shrink as the sky vomits a torrent of snow the likes of which I've never seen. Then a muted jingling sound drifts from the far end of the street.

I lean over the candle, careful not to smother the flame, as I peer down the long stretch of snow-covered pavement, trying to see where the music is coming from. But other than hazy swirls of white, it's impossible to see much of anything.

The candle continues to liquefy as the noise grows increasingly louder until, seemingly out of nowhere, a blaze of color and sound bursts through the haze and a crazy graffiti-covered trolley with "Jingle Bells" blaring from overhead speakers that, strangely enough, are shaped just like antlers skids to a stop right before me.

Definitely not the bus I was waiting for, which is exactly why I stay put.

The front door springs open in a cringe-inducing metal-meets-metal shriek that has me gritting my teeth and willing it to end.

"Heya!" comes a disembodied voice from inside. "What-areyawaitinfor? Climmaboard!" The words all slur together, and I can't make out who said them until there's a break in the snow and I'm staring into the face of some old guy with long white dreadlocks, a red-and-green tie-dyed sweatshirt, and a pair of colorful sweat pants bearing the same Christmas-themed graffiti art that marks the sides of the trolley.

And don't even get me started on his insane glasses, which look more like sunglasses than eyeglasses, except for the spirals that keep going in and out of focus.

It's all I need to see to convince me to do my best to ignore him.

The entire scene stinks of trouble. This is pretty much every warning every mother has ever given her kid rolled into one.

Any second now he'll offer me some ice cream and a peek at the puppies he keeps in the back.[15]

I'd rather take my chances on frostbite.[16]

I wave a hand in dismissal, hoping he'll take the hint and move on. But he continues to sit there, grinning like a lunatic, so I raise my voice over the noise and say, "I'm waiting for *another* bus." Emphasis on *another*.

---

[15] So far there's no sign of either ice cream or puppies.
[16] This is exactly what I should have done.

"Then you better get comfortable." He laughs, the sound coming from the depths of his prominent belly. "I'm the only one allowed to drive tonight, and that's only on account of these glasses. They let me see through the veil." He taps the right lens, causing the spirals to change direction so they look like they're receding into his head. "Big storm's about to come in. *Big*. Didn't ya hear?" Only, the way he says it sounds like *Dinnitchahear?* "Way I see it, you got two options. You ride with me, or you turn into a human snowman. Yours to choose."

I check my phone again—still no service. *What is going on?* Though he's right about the storm. It's definitely what you'd call *big*. I've lived in Greentree my whole entire life, and I've never seen it come down this hard.

I calculate the possibility of my making it home without losing my nose to the cold.

The odds are not in my favor. And frankly, I seriously doubt I can make it back to the store without meeting the same fate.

I imagine my face with a big blank space smack-dab in the middle where my nose used to be.

Also not in my favor.

Still I sit, frozen, watching what remains of my birthday candle as it drips down to nothing.

"C'mon! Whereyawannagota, kid?"

I take a moment to mull the question, and figuring I have nothing to lose, I decide to answer honestly. "To a different, better, much cooler life," I say, watching as the fog of my breath shoots straight for the flame, effectively snuffing the wick, as the snow continues to slam so hard it doesn't even seem like snow anymore.

With nowhere to go from here, I heave a breath of defeat, dump the cupcake in the trash, look straight into those crazy spiral glasses, and nod my consent.[17]

"Welcome aboard." He closes the door behind me. "You just get yerself all settled in, and I'll have you where you want to be in no time."

[17] I don't think I need to say how much I regret that.

9

8:17 P.M.—???

END OF THE LINE

Even though the driver told me to take a seat, I stand before him, digging around in my pockets, searching for a bus pass that probably won't even work on this crazy Christmas trolley, or whatever I'm on, as I start to give my address.

"Fuggedaboutit!" he says, shifting into gear and pulling away from the curb in a sudden, jerky movement that sends me scrambling to regain my balance. "On account of the weather and all, this ride's on me. I know just where to take you."

I'm not sure how I feel about that. Then again, it seems like the least of my concerns, considering the circumstances. And with every step down the aisle, I become more and more convinced I've just volunteered for all kinds of trouble.

The trolley is even crazier on the inside than it was on the outside, with that same graffiti theme painted all over the walls and twinkling red and green Christmas lights lining the ceiling, circling the poles, and draped along the seatbacks.

I slink toward the very last row and take a moment to study the finer points of operating the emergency exit in a way I haven't done since I was a kid and my parents made Holly and me memorize it.

The driver shifts gears, singing "Jingle Bells" along with the trolley sound track all the way through until he switches to "It's the Most Wonderful Time of the Year."

A few choruses in, he lowers the volume and asks how I'm doing, which makes me even more suspicious than I already am.

I mean, let's get real. Despite my reputation as a Brainiac Nerd, I've just made the stupidest decision of my entire life by agreeing to ride with this crazy, sunglasses-wearing stranger driving a bizarre trolley in this insane storm while I huddle in the back, hoping I'll arrive home in one piece. And now he wants to chat.

If Dougall were here, I'd probably view this as an adventure, something we could laugh about later. But Dougall's not here, and I can't even imagine laughing at the mess I've gotten myself into.

Still, I force an enthusiasm I don't really own, saying, "Great!" Best not to let on how I'm really feeling, since everyone knows that crazy people, like animals, can smell fear from a mile away. "But I'll be even better when I arrive in one piece and my bodyguard is waiting for me!"

I don't know why I added that part about the bodyguard. It's not like I have one. Though with the matching Christmas sweater, hat, gloves, and mittens—an ensemble that at my school would surely mark me as bully bait—I definitely look like a person in need of one. I guess I was hoping it would make the driver think twice about messing with me. But he just nods and smiles as though he can't wait to meet him.

I press my nose against the window, allowing my breath to fog up the glass before I wipe it clear with my hand and peer at a landscape so vague and white I can't make any sense of it.

"Hang on, kid," the driver calls, forfeiting a rousing chorus of "Baby, It's Cold Outside." "This storm's about to get wild!"

The next thing I know, the trolley is violently rocking as the snow pounds from all sides, making it impossible to see out the windows.

"I'm feeling thankful for snow grilles right about now, how 'bout you?" The driver laughs, a light, slightly melodic sound that somehow grates on my ears.

And what the heck are snow grilles, anyway?

I check my cell again. No service, same as before.

But the note app still works, so this is the moment I decide to thumb-type everything that took place, exactly as I experienced it, from the moment the trouble started until the moment I decided it was a good idea to accept a ride from a mental hospital escapee.

Provided Crazy Trolley Guy doesn't decide to destroy all the evidence, including my cell phone.

When I finally finish, I close my eyes tightly and pray I'll live long enough to regret this decision.

I stay that way for what feels like forever. Eyes shut. Hands clenched to the point where my fingers go numb. Rocking back and forth like a baby, hoping that just this once, on the undisputed worst day of my life, Lady Luck will do me a solid and get me out of here alive.

I guess I must've fallen asleep, because that's exactly how the driver eventually finds me—a huddled, shivering mess—as he reaches out to grab my arm, his long, gnarled fingers clawing at my shoulder.

"Heya. Wake up, kid. We're here!" He gives me a shake, looming over me and grinning like the lunatic I'm convinced that he is.

I blink one eye open. The other follows. Then I blink them both again, this time adding a head shake and face rub for good measure. But the scene outside my window stays exactly the same.

"Where the heck am I?" I stare at a landscape of sunny skies, a few fluffy white clouds, and miles of palm trees stretching as far as the eye can see. While I may not know where I am, one thing's for sure: this is *not* Greentree. "Where the heck have you taken me?" I glare at him accusingly.

"You're exactly where you wanted to be." The driver heads back down the aisle as though he expects me to follow.

"I asked you to take me *home!*" I shoot eye daggers at his back, outraged in a way I can barely contain.

"Did you?" He stops and glances over his shoulder, lifting his glasses to shoot me a long, hard look before anchoring them in his dreadlocks. "Good luck to ya, kid!" He pulls a lever, and the front door springs open with that same horrible, squeaking protest as before.

"Unh-uh. No way." I shake my head vehemently, fully aware of the irony of how I prayed for the chance to escape, only to get it and refuse to budge from my seat. "I am *not* going out there!"

The driver cocks his head and narrows his eyes, reminding me of Sir Dasher Dashaway when he sees something confusing. "Ride's over, kid. Nowhere to go from here. This is it. The end of the line. Your final stop."

"But you have to take me *back!* Back *home.* To *Greentree.* You can even drop me at that same bus stop, and I'll walk the rest of the way. I don't care how much it's snowing!"

The driver shakes his head, eyes glinting. "That wasn't the deal. I upheld my end, now it's time for you to uphold yours." He motions to the door.

"But I don't even know where I am!" I'm acting panicky, childish, but it's not like I care. The only witness is a lunatic. Besides, I have good reason to panic.

"Ride's over," he repeats. "This is the end of the—"

"Stop saying that!" I check my cell, ready to call my parents, Dougall, 911, even Plum if she can get me out of here, but not only does it no longer have service, it's completely dead, which means I can't even add more evidence to my notes. Which also means, I can't leave any more clues for my parents to find me.

"Can you at least tell me where I am?" I ask, my voice sounding as defeated as I feel.

"Exactly where you wanted to be."

I shake my head, so frustrated I could cry.

"And it looks like that bodyguard you mentioned is waiting, just like you said."

The driver uncurls a long, gnarly finger bearing an even longer, gnarlier fingernail and gestures past the door to a shiny black superstretch limo bearing a personalized license plate that reads ★NICK★. He's the biggest dude I've ever seen and is wearing a black suit and holding a sign reading NICK DASHAWAY.

"That's you, innit?"

"Yeah, but . . ." My voice fades. I have no idea what to say.

"Best not to keep 'em waiting. It's been a pleasure having you on board, though."

He gives me a little nudge that's really more like a shove, and, left with no other option, I make my way down the steps.

"Oh, wait up there, kid. I almost forgot!" He slaps his forehead in a ridiculous, cartoonish way, with his head shaking and eyes rolling. "This is for you."

He thrusts into my hand a piece of paper that looks like

any other ordinary bus ticket except for the sprigs of holly etched around the edges.

"Your return ticket," he tells me. "It's good for five days and five days only. Take good care not to lose it. It's your only way back."

"Can I use it now?" I ask, ready to turn it over and get back to Greentree.

"Nah. You and I are done for today. You just keep it somewhere safe." He rubs his chin, casting a worried glance toward the limo. Then quickly replaces it with a mile-wide grin that exposes every shiny gold tooth in his mouth. "Five days, kid. 'At's all ya got."

I do a quick calculation. "So, Christmas?"

"When Christmas Eve turns to Christmas—one minute past midnight."

I shove the ticket deep into my hoodie's hidden inner pocket, wondering if I'm about to make the same mistake all over again by getting into a car with some guy I don't even know. But when I shoot the driver a pleading look, he just shakes his head and shoves me down the steps into the stifling heat. Not knowing what else to do, I say a little prayer, shield my eyes from the glare, and head for the shiny black limo and the driver holding the sign bearing my name.

DASHING ALL THE WAY

10

5 Days, 11 Hours, 2 Minutes,
and 22 Seconds
till Christmas

WE THREE KINGS

From the looks of it, I'm pretty sure the big hulking guy holding the sign with my name on it is not just a bodyguard but also doubles as the chauffeur. Which would explain the black suit, mirrored sunglasses, and hat.

He also looks strangely familiar.

Not that I actually know anyone with that many muscles who dresses like that, but there's something about his mouth, chin, and jaw (which is pretty much all I can see on account of the glasses and hat) that makes me squint and think, *Hmmm.*

I slow my approach, not entirely sure what I'm about to get myself into. Figuring I should start by introducing myself, maybe saying something like *Hi, I'm Nick Dashaway—the guy on your sign.* Or better yet, *the guy whose name is on your sign,* since it's not like *I'm* on his sign, which is how it sounded before. But I guess I'm overthinking it, because before I can say anything, he's tucking the sign under his arm and swinging the limo door open, checking the inside before motioning for me to climb in.

I slide onto the smooth leather seat and drop my backpack onto the floor between my feet. As my eyes slowly adjust to the darkness I notice the shadowy figure sitting just opposite, with big beefy forearms resting on his knees, slicked-back hair that looks like it's been glued to the sides of his head using one of the sealants from my dad's store, and a set of squinty eyes facing imminent invasion from a pair of unruly brows threatening to overtake them.

And just when I'm about to bolt, it hits me—it's Ezer. Ben Ezer. Josh Frost's manager.

"Nick, what the heck kinda stunt you pulling?" His gaze glints on mine, like we're continuing a conversation I don't remember starting.

My whole face squinches. Clueless doesn't even begin to describe how I feel.

"Keeping us waiting like that." He makes a tongue-clicking-teeth sound, like he's the headmaster and I'm the delinquent student about to be suspended. "You better not be letting your star power go to your head. You've been warned. I won't stand for that kind of thing. Business is business, Nick. You need to keep it professional. Keep your ego in check.

Don't ever forget, I'm your manager, not one of your adoring fans."

Fans?

I glance around the limo, trying to see beyond the tinted windows, but I only end up more confused.

"You're *my* manager?" I gape, sure there's been a mistake.

"Cute." Ezer snickers as he leans back in his seat and steeples his fingers. "Real cute, Nick." He shakes his head once, twice, then sinks a hand deep into his briefcase, only to resurface with a big fat pile of papers he shoves right at me.

"What's this?"

"Contracts—product licenses for that line of sunglasses—that commercial in Japan—your new book deal. We've been over these already. Just sign where I've tagged 'em."

Japan?

But what comes out instead is "I'm writing a book?" Even though I know it's not real—even though I'm pretty sure I fell asleep at that bus stop and have ended up in some kind of bizarre dream—the idea sends me into a panic.

I'm already maxed out on my schoolwork, not to mention the extra-credit projects I've taken on. And now I'm supposed to write a book?

"Don't be ridiculous." Ezer shakes his head like I've said something stupid. "That's what ghostwriters are for. They do all the work. You get all the glory. Now sign."

He wags one of his thick, hot-dog fingers at the mountain of papers piled high on my lap, but all I can do is stare at them with a growing sense of bewilderment.

"What's the hesitation? You've done this a million times already. Nick, I *need* these signed before we get home. The shoot's already been delayed because of you—we can't afford to waste any more time."

I gaze down at the papers, then back at him. "The shoot?"

"Have you been drinking?" He slides to the end of his seat and sticks his face close to mine, his nostrils twitching as he sniffs for fumes.

"I don't think so," I say, wondering if someone slipped me something without my knowing. Maybe that's why I'm stuck in this bizarre otherworld? Maybe Plum's candle let off some kind of hallucinogenic fumes? If I wake up ten hours from now, begging for coffee and aspirin like I once saw Holly do, then I'll know that I'm on to something. But for now I'm as confused as Ezer.

"You don't *think* so." He shakes his head again, like it's some kind of inside joke only he understands. "*Mojo*, Nick. The correct answer is *always* Mojo. You're being paid a pile of money to endorse that brand—don't you forget it."

"Listen," I say, setting the papers aside. "As much as I dreamed of a moment like this, now that it's happening, I'm not all that comfortable. I think there's been some kind of mistake. Even if this is a dream, it's starting to feel really weird."

Ezer rubs his eyes with his knuckles in a way that looks really painful, then sighs long and deep, as though I require the kind of patience he just doesn't own.

"I mean, I clearly heard Josh vote for me and all, but the

last time we spoke, you specifically said I didn't have it. You know, that *thing*, that indefinable thing that makes someone a star. You told me to do myself a favor and find another dream. You said there was nothing wrong with knowing my limits. You said—"

"That right?" He lifts his head and looks at me with eyeballs turned red and spidery around the whites. "I said all of that. To *you*?"

I nod. It's the one thing I know to be true.

"Okay, Nick." He rubs a meaty hand across his face, his fat gold watch practically winking at me. "Here's the thing. I'm tired. It's been a long day—a long day of waiting for *you*, I might add. But if you're feeling insecure and need a little pep talk, just say so. Stop playing games about imaginary conversations that never took place, deal?" He crosses his legs and runs his tongue along a set of teeth so white and straight they look like they fell out of a box of Chiclets. "Here goes." He clears his throat like he's preparing to give a very long monologue. "Nick Dashaway, you are an immensely talented performer. From the first moment I saw you, I knew you were destined to be a star. Sure, you were rough around the edges, but it was nothing a little coaching couldn't fix. Turns out, I was right, and because of it, you are now the biggest teen star in the world. Your endorsements alone have made you a millionaire many times over, females from eight to eighty think you're adorable, and your reality show, *Dashaway Home*, enjoys worldwide syndication. In fact, it's so successful we're about to begin shooting the *Twelve Days of*

Dashaway Christmas Countdown edition, which we're all very excited about. Apparently more excited than you, since we were all on time for the shoot." He takes a deep breath. "That enough? We good here? You feeling pumped enough to do some actual work?"

I stare out the window, taking in a seemingly never-ending stream of mansions, sunshine, palm trees, and a big green-and-white sign that reads TINSEL HILLS, POPULATION 34,000. Though just as we're about to pass, I swear I see the number change to 34,001.

I'm caught in a dream.

There's no other way to explain it.

"Now, if you can please get it together long enough to sign these papers, I'd be forever grateful. We got a show to produce, and we're way behind schedule."

I thumb through the thick wad and try to make sense of what I'm reading. But the print is so tiny, and every single page is written in a language that only lawyers can translate.

This may be a dream, but I'm still not sure I'm willing to sign something legally binding.

"Shouldn't my parents take a look at this first? You know, just to make sure it's okay?"

From the look on Ezer's face, it's pretty much the comment that just might flip his switch.

His features scrunch. His hands grip his knees so tightly it looks like his knuckles are about to burst through his skin. "Your parents? Real funny, Nick. I hope you're enjoying yourself, because trust me, I'm not. Your parents work for you. They're employees of the show. They kept getting in the way, so we had you emancipated. I'm the one who guides you now. So come on, let's get to it already. We're almost home, and the cameras are waiting. Where's that fancy pen I gave you?"

Fancy pen?

The fanciest pen I own is a white plastic one with the green-and-red Dashaway Home and Hardware logo running down the side.

Surely this is the moment when I wake up. As soon as I look for a pen I don't have, the limo, Ezer, the contracts, the Mojo energy drink endorsement, the supposed fans, even the book deal, will be gone in a flash, and I'll find myself half-frozen, half-dead, and probably missing half my nose, still waiting for the bus back in Greentree.

"Front pocket of your backpack, Nick. Hurry! We're two blocks away!"

It's been fun while it lasted.

Sort of.

I take one last look around the limo, one last look at Ezer's annoyed face, and reach inside my bag. My fingers root around for the pencil that's usually there, the one with teeth marks running up and down the sides, when I butt against something smooth and slick. It's one of those really expensive pens, like the kind you see in movies with big-shot lawyers and Wall Street guys closing billion-dollar deals.

This is the most insane dream I've ever had.

"Great," Ezer snaps, snatching the papers out of my hand and shoving them back inside his briefcase. "We're home. You need to get into wardrobe and makeup, ASAP. You can sign these tomorrow."

11

HOLLY JOLLY

"Nick! Nick—over here! Give us a smile, Nick!"

The second we turn onto the next street, we're bombarded by paparazzi shouting my name, banging on the limo doors, the windows, the roof, all of them chasing alongside us.

They beg me to stop, pose, answer questions—but when I start to lower the window, Ezer slaps a hand over mine and puts it back up.

"You kidding me? When's the last time you looked in the mirror?" He shakes his head. "You're seriously willing to be photographed in *that*?"

I gaze down at my mom's Christmas creation, instantly overcome by a flood of shame.

Partly because Ezer's right, the sweater is hideous.

And partly because my mom made it with good intentions and thinking about how hideous it is makes me feel guilty.

"I don't know what you've been up to, but we're going to get you cleaned up and pretend this whole thing never happened." He frowns so deeply you could call it a grimace and not be exaggerating.

We turn into a long, winding drive bordered with palm trees, flowers, and hedges. The big iron gates close behind us, keeping the paparazzi out, but that doesn't stop them from pushing their telephoto lenses through the bars, snapping pictures nonstop. And the next thing I know, Ezer is dragging me out of the limo and ushering me into an air-conditioned mansion he insists belongs to me, no matter how improbable that seems.

"Why don't you head up and change, then get yourself over to hair and makeup so we can start shooting? Sound good?" He slips his cell phone from his pocket and starts to move away.

"Head *up*?" I glance around helplessly, taking in the walls covered with giant paintings of brightly colored blobs and shapes, the ginormous crystal chandelier hanging overhead that's practically daring you to stand directly beneath its sharp, daggerlike spikes, the round glass table with no other purpose than holding a large vase of flowers—and that's just the entryway.

"Nick, I'm gonna be honest here." Ezer's voice is so irritated I can't help but flinch. "This little game of yours stopped being funny long before it started. So, please, I'm begging you, get to your room and start the process of reinventing yourself. You got an entire crew waiting on you, and I'm sure they'd all appreciate you getting your act together so they can get home before midnight." He motions toward a large, wide staircase with metal rods standing in for banisters. "When you're ready, meet us in the kitchen so we can shoot the cookie scene. Nick? You following?"

"I don't bake," I say, cringing when I see the face that he makes.

"No kidding." He shakes his head and mutters something under his breath, then points toward the staircase. "Today, Nick."

I take the stairs two at a time, acting on Ezer's need to see me hurry, even though I have no idea where I'm going. And despite my being a huge celebrity with a global fan base, the people who pass me on their way down are too busy shouting into their headsets to be of any help.

When I reach the landing, I gaze down a long hall with chalky white walls covered with more giant paintings of brightly colored blobs and a bunch of doors that most likely lead to bedrooms, but which one is mine?

In Greentree my parents' room is at the far end, so I figure I'll start with the door closest to me, just to my right. This may be nothing at all like the house I grew up in, but there's usually some sort of pattern all houses follow to keep people from getting lost.

I knock on the door, then instantly feel really stupid.

If it's my door, then clearly there's no need to knock. Still, there's no way to be sure it's my door until I open it, and the last thing I want to do is guess wrong and walk in on something completely embarrassing.

"Nick—hey! There you are. We've been looking everywhere for you. We're all so worried. You okay?"

The voice is familiar, but the words are spoken with such genuine relief at seeing me that I have to turn around to be sure it really is her. And what I see makes my eyes practically pop out of my head.

This is not the Holly I know and loathe.

This Holly is so different, all I can do is stand there and stare.

For starters, the wavy dark hair that's always hanging in her face has been replaced with fluffy golden waves that sort of bounce and swirl like she's a walking, talking shampoo commercial.

And instead of ghostly pale skin, this Holly looks healthy, like she actually spends time outdoors.

And don't even get me started on the pink dress and heels.

It's like a bizarre, alternate-universe, Barbie doll version of Holly. It's as though the sarcastic part of her brain has been surgically removed and replaced with the impulse to grin.

Holly's hand presses between my shoulders and steers me toward a spacious room at the very end of the hallway with solid double doors, miles of carpet, and a giant round bed smack in the center. "Better change quick. You know how Ezer gets."

She pushes into the room, picks up a pile of clothes from the bed, and places them in my arms. "I'd really appreciate it if we could get started soon. Remember that audition I told you about? It's today. Wish me luck!"

Audition? Since when does Holly ever audition for anything other than the role of "most annoying sister," which she nailed long ago?

But when I look at her again, standing before me with a bright and hopeful expression, all I can do is mutter, "Um, okay. Good luck," then watch as she exits as quickly as she appeared, leaving me to sink onto the soft furry blanket I hope isn't from a real animal skin as I check out my room.

It's just as modern up here as it is downstairs. The carpet is white, which seems really impractical, but from the looks of it, someone's doing a good job with the vacuuming. The shelves along the far wall resemble long metal slats floating in space, and they're crammed with all kinds of awards and framed photos of me posing with some big-time celebrities and musicians. Including one of me standing next to the president, both of us wearing grins so big it's like we're in a smiling contest. The desk facing the window is made from some kind of thick, clear plastic that juts right out of the wall, yet it still manages to support a pile of just about every electronic gadget you could possibly want. There's a large bathroom off to the right and a huge walk-in closet next to that. And I swear, if you squished those two rooms together, they'd be bigger than all of our bedrooms at home combined.

This dream is so detailed, it's almost like there's a set decorator standing by.

And yeah, despite my not waking up during the whole fancy-pen incident, I'm still holding to the dream theory. There's no other way to explain it.

I dump the contents of my backpack onto my bed, but instead of the books I usually haul around, it's filled with all kinds of stuff that's not mine.

For starters, there's a bunch of grooming stuff I would never use in real life, like a bottle of oil you're supposed to put on your face and a jar of something called Dashaway Do that's supposed to be a kind of hair paste, like I have my own hair product line. There's even a small tube of lip gloss that definitely, one hundred percent, isn't mine.

A black leather wallet crammed with fat wads of hundred-dollar bills and loads of black and silver credit cards sits there as well.

The rest is more normal—a comb, a brush, a small mirror. Well, normal for the kind of person who spends most of the time thinking about his appearance.

I change into the clothes Holly gave me and am just about to shove the wallet (since my name is on the cards, and considering this is a dream and all, I might as well put them to use, right?) and my cell phone (in case it starts working) into the back pocket of the designer jeans when Ezer shouts from the other side of the door, "Do not make me come in there, Nick. I'm serious. I—"

But before he can finish, I open the door and push past him. In search of whoever's in charge of hair and makeup. I mean, if I'm going to dream I'm an International Superstar, I might as well enjoy some of the perks before I wake up.

TWITTER LIPS

I end up in a den that's not at all like a normal den.

And by *not at all normal,* I mean it's not like my Greentree den.

Which means it's a really, really cool den.

The kind of den you might see on an old episode of *MTV Cribs.*

There's a flat-screen TV that practically covers an entire wall; an oversized U-shaped couch that looks really comfortable; a long, skinny, rectangular fireplace set into the middle of the wall with small broken-up pieces of glass instead of the fake wooden logs you usually see; a bar stocked with Mojo, the energy drink Ezer said I'm endorsing; a killer sound system; and a version of Xbox that's not even out yet.

I barely have a chance to take it all in when some lady with bright-red hair and matching lips waves me over and tells me to take a seat.

"Your skin looks good." She pinches my chin between her forefinger and thumb, twisting my head back and forth, inspecting me like she's a doctor or something. "You been using that oil sample I gave you?"

She squints, waits for me to reply, pinching my chin even harder every second I make her wait for the answer.

"Um, yeah. I guess." I bat her fingers away.

She laughs under her breath and starts messing with a pile of brushes, powders, and other unidentifiable gunk. "Well, whatever you're doing, it's working. And I'm glad to see you're heeding my advice to stay out of the sun. I'm expecting you to send me a thank-you card on your thirtieth birthday." She laughs even harder. Guess she's easily amused. "Anyway, you don't need much. Maybe just a little concealer around the eyes, a dash of powder on the nose and cheeks to keep you from getting too shiny, a little liner to make those hazel eyes pop, then we'll finish with a dot of gloss right in the center of your bottom lip like we did last time. Sound good?"

She comes at me wielding a small brush dipped in beige glop, but my first and only instinct is to fend her off. "I wear lip gloss?" I hold my hands up in front of me, protecting my face from impending assault.

"Your lips were trending on Twitter. Girls ages ten to fourteen loved them, and I aim to please! Now, hold still— don't make this take any longer than it needs to."

This time when she comes at me, I close my eyes and surrender. It's only a dream. Not like anyone in Greentree will see me wearing makeup, so why not go along and see where it leads? And when she sticks a mirror in my face and tells me to look, I see a shiny-lipped, powdered-down version of me staring back.

"Okay, handsome, let's get you over to hair." She spins the barstool until I'm face to face with a heavily tattooed, multipierced guy who's quite possibly wearing more makeup than Holly and me combined.

"I promise, this won't hurt a bit!" He laughs, coming at me with a comb in one hand and a can of hairspray in the other. And the only thing I can do under the circumstances is sit back and wait for it to be over.

★

By the time I'm herded into the kitchen, everyone's so busy adjusting the cameras and lighting that no one pays me much notice, which is kind of a relief, since it gives me a moment to take in the scene.

If I thought Holly looked like some bizarre Barbie doll version of herself, it's nothing compared to my mom, who looks like Holly's bizarre Barbie sister. Older sister, but still, it's like there's only a few years between them. Like they might share a closet, makeup tips, maybe even ex-boyfriends.

The only reason I even recognize her as my mom is because that's what Holly called her—except she didn't actually call her Mom, she called her Eileen. And since Eileen is my mom's name back in Greentree, I figure it's safe to assume it's my mom's name here too.

Though I have to admit I like the idea of calling my mom by her first name. It's something I'd never get away with back home. Besides, it's impossible for me to refer to her as Mom when she doesn't look like she could be anyone's mom.

The Greentree version of my mom is usually so oblivious to her appearance that most of the time it's all she can do to get out of the house wearing matching shoes.

This version clearly takes the job very seriously.

My mom looks like one of those super-rich ladies who spend most of their time bouncing between hair salons, shopping malls, and gyms.

My mom looks like Mrs. Turtledove if Mrs. Turtledove was blond, tan, and had a body that's been weirdly compressed in some places and blown up in others.

Back in Greentree Mrs. Turtledove is the only person I know who even tries to resemble a rich Hollywood lady. But now, after seeing the real deal in front of me, Mrs. Turtledove doesn't even come close.

"Nick—hi, Nick!" My mom, Eileen, calls to me in this unfamiliar, superfriendly way. I mean, don't get me wrong, my mom is always friendly, but this is a different kind of friendly. She's acting more like we're BFFs than mother and son, the way her eyes get all big and excited and her hand windshield-wipes back and forth in the same kind of wave Tinsley Barnes and her popular friends use on each other.

"Nick! Finally!" Ezer snaps, his tone causing Eileen to jump to my defense.

"Don't talk to Nicky like that," she scolds.

Nicky?

Since when does my mom call me Nicky?

Nick, pretty much always.

Nicholas when she's mad.

But never, ever *Nicky.*

Not even when I was a baby.

"I'm sure he has a very good reason for his tardiness." She flashes a grin so supportive that, even though I'm surprised to hear her say that, I instinctively grin in return. My Greentree mom doesn't tolerate tardiness, and I always kind of wish she'd lighten up and stop making such a big thing over little delays.

When I see my dad, Joe, well, compared to Eileen's and Holly's, his transformation isn't nearly as dramatic, but that's not to say he looks anything even remotely like my Greentree dad.

The forehead creases I've grown used to seeing look like they've been pressed with an iron. And when he flashes me a nod and a grin from across the room, I can't help but notice how the gray patches in his hair are now blond, like someone took a paintbrush, dipped it in yellow, and covered those parts.

He looks like the kind of dad who spends a lot of time at board meetings and on swanky golf courses—the sort of person who's considered far too important to ever set foot inside a place like Dashaway Home and Hardware. He'd send one of his many assistants instead.

Though his eyes are still like mine. Only a lot less stressed, which is really nice to see.

He waves from his mark.

I wave back.

And with the cameras in place, and the kitchen counters and island overflowing with multiple trays of freshly baked cookies, along with all the necessary decorating tools, the director shouts, "*Twelve Days of Dashaway Christmas Countdown.* Day one—scene one—take one!" and immediately snaps that black-and-white clapper board thing, which, according to the briefing sheet Ezer handed me when my clothes were being inspected for stray pieces of lint, means it's my job to move toward my mark and hug Eileen, high-five Joe, and compliment Holly on her necklace so she can balance it on the tip of her index finger, aim it toward the camera, and mention the name of the shop where she bought it. Then I lean down to pet my dog, Sir Dasher Dashaway, who, also according to the notes, will run into the room right on cue, where he will join Holly and me as we decorate cookies like the world's favorite (and most famous!) brother-and-sister act while our parents look on adoringly.

It all seems simple enough, which is why it goes exactly as planned.

Until Sir Dasher Dashaway runs into the room and my jaw falls to my knees as my eyeballs bug out like they're loaded on springs.

"What *happened*?" I groan, so shocked by the sight of him I forgot that the cameras were rolling. But *sheesh!* While the celebrity makeover looks good on my parents and Holly, when it comes to Sir Dasher Dashaway, it's completely over the top.

The Greentree version of Sir Dasher Dashaway is what you might call more beautiful inside than out. He's a one-eyed rescue mutt of indeterminate origins with oversized paws, black-and-white fur with the occasional brown spot, floppy ears, and a stub for a tail.

The celebrity version is a tiny white overgroomed, over-pedigreed beast whose natural habitat is the inside pocket of an expensive designer purse.

"Cut!" the director shouts as everything that was once set in motion comes to a screeching halt.

"Is there a problem, Nick?" Ezer shoots me a look not unlike the ones from the limo.

"I—" I look all around. Everyone is staring, waiting for me to explain.

"Nick?" Ezer lifts a brow and flips his palms so they're sunny-side up. A silent ultimatum if I've ever seen one.

"No. Um." I swallow, take another look at Sir Dasher Dashaway, and try to make peace with the horrible sight of him. But it's too much to ask, so I turn away and say, "I'm good. We're good. Let's shoot."

I head back to my mark as the director calls, "*Twelve Days of Dashaway Christmas Countdown.* Day one—scene one—take two. From the top!"

COOKIE CUTTER

We're in the middle of shooting the last scene of the day, the one where Holly "accidentally" decorates my cheek with a blob of frosting so I can retaliate by drawing a red-icing mustache on her face. And while that's going down, Sir Dasher Dashaway will, right on cue, jump onto the counter and eat a bunch of the cookies when we're not looking, only to have my parents walk into the room and—instead of getting upset like most parents would—throw their hands up and join in the fun.

I don't think I need to explain how not a single thing about this reality show is even the slightest bit real.

Every "spontaneous" moment is carefully scripted.

Including the concealed ramp tiny Sir Dasher Dashaway needs to "jump" onto the kitchen counter.

While I'm sure the edited version will portray just the amount of lighthearted fun the audience loves, the actual reality is that Holly had an allergic reaction to the icing that made her face swell up and turn red, and Sir Dasher Dashaway ate so many cookies he vomited all over the floor and had to be replaced with a stunt dog who I'm told regularly stands in as his double.

From what I've learned so far, acting "real" for a reality show is so exhausting I'm starting to wonder if I had it all wrong about how great it would be to live a life like Josh Frost's.

Oh, and did I mention that we're on our thirteenth take?

But who's counting?

I'm just about to call "Cut" on this dream, thank everyone for participating, and find a way to wake up and get back to my normally scheduled life, when Tinsley Barnes enters.

The *same* Tinsley Barnes from back in Greentree.

Only better, if you can believe it.

Her hair looks like it's been washed with melted-down gold bars.

Her eyes resemble two very rare sapphires.

And as for her body, well, let's just say it's a little more . . . *exaggerated* in all the right places.

But what really stands out is the way this new Tinsley looks at me.

And by that I mean she actually *looks* at me.

Like, on purpose.

As though it wasn't some horrible accident she instantly regrets.

I take a steadying breath and force myself to return the look. Only to see her lips lift at the sides as she switches her gaze to her shoes.

"Nick—wake up! You're on!" the director calls, which is kind of embarrassing, since he caught me in the act of staring at Tinsley. But now that I've got an audience I actually care about, well, I put on a performance so good, the next words out of his mouth are "And . . . cut! That's a wrap!"

Everyone springs into action, dismantling the lights and cameras in a way so frenzied it reminds me of the moment when the final bell rings back at Greentree. Which of course gets me thinking about Dougall—the one person who has yet to make an appearance (other than Plum, who clearly has no place in this dream), and it's kind of too bad, because it might be fun to see him looking like a celebrity.

I unhook my mike, toss it onto the counter, and make a beeline for Ezer. Not that I have anything important to say, but since Tinsley's standing beside him, it's pretty much all the incentive I need.

Also, it'll give me a chance to make sure she really did look at me in the way that I think, because if it turns out I'm right, I may not be in such a hurry to wake up from this dream.

Ezer looks at me but doesn't say anything, which makes it kind of awkward, since I don't know what to say either. So

I end up standing there like an idiot, shuffling from foot to foot while trying not to stare too hard at Tinsley.

Despite repeatedly reminding myself that in this particular place and time I'm an International Superstar, I'm so used to being a dork that deep down I still feel like one.

Which means I still act like one.

"You remember Tinsley?" Ezer finally says after a long, painful silence. "I think you met a few years back. She's one of your biggest fans." He pats her on the shoulder. "She's got a great set of pipes too. Maybe you two could collaborate sometime?"

I lift my gaze just as Tinsley lifts hers, her deep blue eyes meeting mine as I croak out something that sounds vaguely like "Sure, anytime," while the dork who lives deep down inside dances like Snoopy when Charlie Brown puts food in his bowl.

Tinsley blushes, like a wave of pink has splashed over her cheeks. And knowing it's all because of me pretty much makes this the best moment of my entire life.

"Great." Ezer grins, looking the happiest I've seen him all day. "I've got a few songs in mind. Maybe you two can take a look?"

I nod like I'm okay either way, but deep down inside the happy dance continues.

"Nick, you're clear for the rest of the day, and Tinsley, you have some time to spare."

"Up to you." Tinsley pulls her shoulders in and clasps

her hands to her lap as she sways from side to side. It's a move I've seen her pull countless times in Greentree when she's talking to Mac Turtledove, only now she's doing it for me.

"Yeah. Sure. Why not?" I shrug like the International Superstar that I am. Trying not to hyperventilate when Tinsley moves so close there's only a few inches between us.

"I'm so honored you're willing to take a chance on me." The blush of her cheeks deepens in a way that's impossible to resist. "I know how busy you are."

I keep my cool and just nod in return, as if to say: *My life as an International Superstar keeps me incredibly busy, but I always have time for a fan like you.*

"I know Uncle Ezer would love to get something recorded for the final Christmas episode, but again, it's yours to decide, Nick."

The first thing I think is *Tinsley's related to Ezer?*

Though it's quickly replaced with *Tinsley Barnes knows my name!*

She looks to Ezer for confirmation, the two of them exchanging a look I can't read, but who cares?

Recording a song together means spending *a lot* of time together.

Just when I thought I was ready to bail, this dream takes a turn that definitely makes it worth living.

"Why don't you two head out to the pool?" Ezer says. "I'll have Lisa bring you some drinks."

I have a pool?

Cool!

And though I have no idea where it is, that doesn't stop me from leading Tinsley toward a sliding glass door I hope leads to my backyard, opening it wide as I say, "After you."

14

ALL THE SMOOTH MOVES

Turns out, my backyard is an exact replica of a tropical paradise.

Not that I've ever been to a tropical paradise, but it's the kind of backyard you'd expect to find in Hawaii, Tahiti, or even L.A.

But I could just as easily be smacked down in the middle of Antarctica, and I'd be just as happy.

With Tinsley sitting beside me, her feet dangling in the water, a pile of potential songs resting between us—well, the grove of palm trees, the giant pool with the lazy river, the three waterfalls, the swim-up bar, the Jacuzzi, the fake beach, and the grotto all pale in comparison.

I try not to stare, to just focus on the pile of songs. But

it's hard to concentrate on much of anything when Tinsley's eyes go all pretty and squinty and her voice lilts in this adorable way as she hums the tunes to herself.

"What do you think of this one?" She looks up just in time to catch me staring, so I quickly shift my focus to the sheet of music she's holding.

"Um, yeah," I say, not wanting to let on that here, like in Greentree, I have no idea how to read music.

"Should we try it?" she asks. "You know, just for fun?"

"Sure, but you start and I'll join in," I'm quick to say, hoping to cover the fact that I have no idea how to begin.

The second she starts singing, it's like everything else ceases to exist. Ezer was right. Tinsley's "pipes" are incredible. Her voice is soft yet strong, mesmerizing and sure. Which is strange, because that is the one flaw of the Greentree Tinsley. If the last few years of talent shows and school plays are anything to go by, her singing voice is the worst.

She shoots me a sideways glance, waiting for me to join in. While I'm not really sure how this will go, I clear my throat, hope for the best, and join her.

And the truth is, I sound awful.

Like really, truly awful.

So awful Tinsley actually loses her place, and I'm pretty sure this is the moment when the dream falls apart.

Except I keep singing, keep plowing through, and after a bit, while it's nowhere near great, it's good enough to finish the song and not ruin it completely.

"That was a little rough." She laughs. "I guess we should've warmed up."

Nice of Tinsley to include herself in the blame, but I think we both know I sounded like a frog dying of heatstroke.

"Still, it has potential—don't you think?" Her eyes get all gleamy as she reaches toward me and places the tips of her fingers on the top of my knee. "But it's really up to you, Nick. What do you think—should we try it again?"

What do I think?

I think: *Tinsley Barnes has her hand on my knee! Tinsley Barnes is actually, on purpose, engaging in physical contact with me!*

What I say is "Yeah, I can see its potential," in a voice so hoarse I have to clear it three times to get it back to normal.

Still, it doesn't seem to stop her from keeping her hand on my knee and giving it a little squeeze.

It's all I can do to keep my cool as I wipe my palm discreetly down the leg of my jeans, making sure it'll be nice and dry when I place it over Tinsley's hand.

Which is exactly what I'm about to do when someone creeps up from behind and says, "Lisa told me to bring these to you."

The hand that was veering toward Tinsley's falls limp to my side as my vision goes in and out of focus, barely comprehending what I'm seeing, despite the alarm in my head. *Plum!*

Even in my one perfect dream, in my one perfect moment, Plum Bailey manages to show up and ruin everything.

And the weird thing is, she looks just as out of place as the old Plum—only different.

Instead of being blond and tan like everyone else around here, she's as pale as ever and dressed mostly in black, with hair dyed to match. Also, the braces are gone, leaving a set of perfectly straight white teeth in their wake. She's like an edgy, alternative version of Plum, and yet she's still clearly Plum.

Tinsley starts checking her cell phone while Plum lifts two frosty glasses of lemonade from her tray and places them beside us.

Her stubby, black-painted nails impatiently drum the side of her leg as she meets my gaze long enough to ask, "Do you need anything else?"

The question is simple. One I should be able to answer without hesitation. And yet I'm so upset by her appearance, not to mention the possibility that she might actually work for me, that all I can do is sit there and stare.

I can't afford to have Plum hanging around, fawning all over me.

She'll only get in the way.

But I must've stared for too long, because the next thing I know, Tinsley's getting to her feet, saying, "Um, I think I should leave," as she shoots an unreadable look between Plum and me.

"What? No, don't go!" I say, veering so far from cool, I would be embarrassed if I wasn't so desperate. "She's just—" I jab a thumb toward Plum, having no idea how to finish that thought. I know who she is in Greentree, but I have no idea who she is here.

Plum scowls, heaves a loud, overly dramatic sigh, and storms toward the house like she can't get away from us quickly enough.

I turn back to Tinsley, having no idea what just happened, but I'm fully prepared to beg her to stay if that's what it takes, when I see she's not the one who misunderstood. I did.

Crossing the lawn, making his way to the pool, is a guy who looks a lot like Mac Turtledove.

But that's only because he is Mac Turtledove.

And from the way he and Tinsley look at each other, well, it's clear he's the reason she's in such a hurry to leave.

Her face lights up when she sees him, then she turns to me and says, "If you're up for it, I'll ask Ezer to set up some studio time."

The best I can do is shrug and pretend not to care either way, my brain hijacked by the thought that my dream has just turned into a nightmare.

Like Tinsley's, Mac's makeover is more a matter of adding a few enhancements, as opposed to big, major changes like my parents and Holly got.

Then again, as with Tinsley, there wasn't much to improve.

Still, the differences are right there for anyone to see.

Like the extra inches added to his height.

The additional muscles that seem like they're glued on top of the ones he already had.

And the undeniable haze of cool that announces itself from afar.

And the worst part is, it's not like he actually needed any of that.

"Hey, babe." He snakes a hand around Tinsley's waist and pulls her close to his side. And the way she smiles in response makes me wonder if this is maybe her dream and not mine.

Tinsley hugs the pile of songs to her chest, looking a little uncomfortable when she says, "Nick, Mac. Mac, Nick," her beautiful head bobbing toward each of us.

"Nice spread." Mac surveys my yard like he's planning for the day when he'll live somewhere bigger, better, a place where Tinsley will never want to leave.

"So—" Tinsley pauses in a way that could be adorable under different circumstances. "See you soon?"

I nod, hoping to appear noncommittal, but nobody's fooled. And if that wasn't enough, I then decide to reach into my pocket and pretend to check the messages on a cell phone that no longer works.

And don't think they don't notice that too.

Make that smooth move number two.

When they're finally gone, I retrace my steps back to my house and go in search of one of the gazillions of people who seem to work for me so I can ask them to brew up a strong pot of coffee.

It's time to wake up.

STARBUCKS EXPRESS

First thing I see when I head into the kitchen is Plum talking to Dougall.

Only it takes me a moment to realize it's Dougall.

Mostly because he looks like the kind of Hollywood hipster who wouldn't know the first thing about Bigfoot, UFOs, or wormholes.

His usual Einstein-fro is now tamed, he's wearing dark skinny jeans that look a lot like mine, and there's a black leather cord hanging from his neck with a silver skull attached to the end. With his multipierced ears covered with small silver hoops and his black V-neck tee clinging to a set of muscles the Greentree version of Dougall doesn't own, he's definitely tied with Sir Dasher Dashaway for the prize of Most Surprising Makeover.

"Hey, Nick." He glances toward me in a way that causes his hair to sweep over his eyes.

I nod, but only barely. Sure, it's kind of cool to see my best friend since third grade looking like an off-duty movie star, which is exactly how I wanted him to look. I mean, if he'd dressed like that back in Greentree, we would've easily clinched our popularity. But here in Tinsel Hills, where nearly everyone seems to work with a stylist, it does nothing to help me. All I care about now is getting a triple shot of caffeine so I can wake up.

Getting eclipsed by Mac Turtledove in real life is one thing—in a dream it's just cruel.

"Coffee. Where can I get some?" I direct the question at Plum, since she seems so at home in my kitchen.

She lifts her gaze from her magazine as though it requires every ounce of effort just to acknowledge my presence. "My mom will be back in a minute. She ran out to the store to food-shop for you." Her voice is as full of contempt as her face.

I stand there, stunned, not knowing what surprises me more: the fact that she really, really (and I mean *really*) seems to hate me or that she just mentioned her mom buying my food.

But then I remember that Plum's mom is named Lisa, so I'm guessing it's the same Lisa who told her to deliver lemonade to Tinsley and me. She probably works as my personal chef or something. Which is kind of cool if you think about it—having a personal chef, I mean.

Still, because of it, Plum probably spends a lot of time hanging around my house resenting the heck out of me, and I can't understand why I'd include something as awful as that in my dream.

Except for maybe the fact that I've always hoped Plum would stop liking me so much.

Which, if that's the case, then I guess it could count as another wish come true.

Thing is, if my wishes are all coming true, then I ask yet again: *Why is Mac Turtledove here?*

"You have a need for caffeine, we'll hit a Starbucks, bro." Dougall pushes a hand through his hair and moves away from the counter as though it's decided.

"There's a Starbucks?" I search for a camera, wondering if it's more product placement, like with Holly's necklace.

This dream brought to you by Tiffany's silver heart necklace and Starbucks' Venti Caramel Frappuccino!

Just one day on the set of my reality show and I'm already becoming jaded and cynical.

"Yeah, right, pick a corner, any corner." Dougall shakes his head and laughs like I made a joke as Plum flips through her magazine, scowling at a picture of me, only to settle on one of some skinny tattooed singer with a pained expression on his face, looking as though she'd be perfectly happy gazing at him for the rest of eternity.

"Plum, you coming?" Dougall asks, before I can stop him.

She just laughs and rolls her eyes.

"Next time," he says, which only makes her laugh again.

"How far of a walk is it?" I'm trying to decide whether or not to bring a jacket.

"Walk?" Dougall looks at me like I said something crazy. "Ha! Good one." He shakes his head and exchanges a look with Plum that's clearly at my expense. "Why would we walk when Sparks loves driving us around?"

"Sparks?" Unfortunately I said it out loud, question mark included.

That's why the chauffeur/bodyguard seemed so familiar— he looked like Sparks! If Sparks grew about a foot, lost a few inches of neck, and added a hundred pounds of solid muscle to his frame.

"Yeah. Of course. Sparks." I try to cover but fail miserably. "I'll just, um . . . I'll just go and . . . tell Sparks to get the limo ready." I pretty much bolt from the room so I won't have to see the looks on their faces.

I'm not fast enough to miss the sound of them laughing.

EARLY RETIREMENT

"Dude, I swear, I don't know how she does it, but every time I see her, she just gets better and better." Dougall stretches across the long leather seat, feet propped near the dark-tinted window, turning the back of my limo into his own portable living room.

"Who?" I shut the divider separating us from Sparks. Partly so he can't eavesdrop on our conversation, but mostly so I'll stop staring at him. It's so weird to see him looking all beefy like that.

"*Who?*" Dougall shakes his head as he takes out his phone and fields a couple texts. "Whaddya mean, *who?* Plum Bailey, that's *who!*"

I lean back against my seat, trying to make sense of it.

Sure, this version of Plum is a slightly better (if not slightly scarier) improvement over the Greentree Plum, but still, he can't be serious, can he?

Does this mean the *real* Dougall back in Greentree has a *real* but secret crush on the *real* Plum? Is that why he insists on encouraging her to hang around like we're still in the third grade and thinks it's perfectly okay to be friends with people like her? Has he liked her that whole entire time without telling me?

I study him closely, trying to figure the odds, and instantly decide against it. The Greentree Dougall is immune to girls. This new version just must have really weird taste.

"I don't know how you can contain yourself, being around her all day. She's so aloof. Thinks she's so much better than us. It drives me crazy!"

"She does? Plum Bailey thinks she's better than us?"

Dougall abandons his phone long enough to grab a frosty can of Mojo from the refrigerated slot that runs along the side of the seats. It's the only thing available, other than water, and I can't help but wonder if I get them for free, since, according to Ezer, they pay me a lot of money to endorse them.

He flips the tab and takes a long sip. "Um, yeah." He swipes the back of his hand across his lips. "I hate to break it to you, but she totally considers you the worst kind of sellout."

"What—why? Because I don't cover half my face with tattoos and black eyeliner?" I shake my head and roll my eyes.

Leave it to Plum to not understand that I'm trying to *inspire* people with my music, not *frighten* them like the skinny rocker dude she was drooling over.

"No, because she thinks your music is 'manufactured, inauthentic crap'—her words. She was just explaining her theory in depth when you walked in."

I frown. I can't help it. Even if I don't give a flying flip about Plum, no one likes a bad review.

"Whatever, bro." Dougall shrugs. "Let the haters hate. You're crying all the way to the bank! Am I right, or am I right?"

He leans across the seat, attempting a fist bump, and even though I'm not really feeling it, I return it with as much faked enthusiasm as I can manage.

For the rest of the ride, Dougall stays glued to his phone as I stare out the window, trying to make sense of a world where palm trees are wrapped with red and white Christmas lights so they look like candy canes, and Plum Bailey shuns me instead of me shunning her. And when Sparks pulls into a Starbucks drive-thru, mumbling something about maintaining my privacy and not causing a scene by actually going inside and standing in line, all I know is that the limo barely fits in the lane. But Sparks is a pro, and before we know it, Dougall and I are sipping for free thanks to the girl working the window who totally freaked when I popped through the sunroof and waved.

I might as well enjoy the good parts of the dream while they're there for the taking.

Then again, for the very first time it occurs to me that if this is a dream, that means I fell asleep on the bus-stop bench, and if I don't wake up soon, I'll probably end up freezing to death.

"Nice move." Dougall pulls his straw from the slot and starts gnawing on the end. "When's the last time you actually paid for one of these, or anything else, for that matter?"

"Well, I did sign her arm. Seems like a fair trade, right?" I blow little puffs of air at the top of my cup and take a tentative first sip that's so bad I can't help but gag.

"You serious about not putting milk or sweetener in that?" Dougall wags his straw at my drink. "Dude, that's a quintuple shot. That's one serious brew you got there."

"I don't want to dilute it," I say, having no idea if that's even possible, since it's not like I'm a regular coffee drinker. In fact, I can't stand the stuff. But I figure it's the best and quickest way to wake up, which I'm still determined to do, since I already tried pinching myself. I mean, it's either that or death by hypothermia.

I force another sip. A few more follow. Fully aware that the sooner I empty this cup, the sooner I'll be back on that frozen Greentree bus stop bench. Most likely frostbitten, but at least it gives me something to work with as opposed to outright dead.

"Jonah's hosting a party." Dougall shows me his phone, and I squint at a long row of texts I can't read. "Do you think we should go?"

His expression turns serious, like this is something to be

carefully debated and considered. But all I can do is wonder if the Jonah he's talking about is *Jonah*, as in the Superfamous Model/Actor Jonah Who's on Every Magazine Cover.

"Then again, his last party was kind of lame. Not sure we should chance that again." Dougall taps his chin with his straw, staring hard at the screen, as though the answer might be hidden somewhere.

I nod like I remember the lame party and take another sip, waiting for the moment the caffeine will take effect.

"Then again, he is calling it *An Aloha Christmas*! And he clearly states that it's a luau theme. All of which is pretty genius, if you think about it. It practically requires every girl to show up wearing a grass skirt and a bikini. . . ." He shoots me a sideways look. "Kinda hard to snub an invite like that. Am I right, or am I right?"

He leans in for another fist bump, but I'm really kind of over it, so I segue into the conversation I'd much rather have. "Speaking of, um, hot girls . . . what do you know about Tinsley Barnes?"

Dougall squints. "Ezer's daughter?"

"Niece."

He thinks harder, eyes narrowing so much they're nearly invisible. "Yeah, she's hot. She's no Plum Bailey. But yeah, I can see it." He focuses back on his phone as though the conversation is over, but I'm just getting started.

"Yeah, but what do we *know* about her? You know, other than her indisputable hotness and all."

"We?"

"You. Me. We. Whatever. Who *is* she exactly?"

"You mean aside from the obvious—a hot girl who lives with Ezer?" Dougall frowns, as though asking him to make the switch to something a little more substantial than his internal hotness scale is going too far.

"Yeah. Like, what's her story? What are her interests? Is she dating anyone?" The last bit is presented like an afterthought, not all that important and definitely not my main reason for mentioning her.

Dougall's expression now borders on annoyed. "I don't know, dude. Why don't you ask Ezer?"

"Because I can't."

He looks at me.

"You know how Ezer gets. He's all over my case," I say, since I can't exactly explain the truth: that I'm starting to feel the effects of my quintuple shot, which means I won't be long in this dream world and none of this will matter anyway.

Dougall laughs and abandons his phone. *Finally.*

"We're doing a song together," I tell him. "Tinsley and me."

I like the way it sounds—*Tinsley and me.* So in my head I say it again.

"You serious? You think that's a good career move?"

I'm taken aback by the question. Honestly, I hadn't even thought of that. All I could think about was having a legitimate reason to spend time with Tinsley. Everything else seemed irrelevant.

"You don't? Think it's a good career move, I mean?"

"I think you're playing right into what Plum was going on about. They'll view you as being even softer than you already are." He smirks. "Then again, it's guaranteed to bring in some solid bank. People always love a duet. And if you make it sappy enough, your existing fans will be happy."

Bank.

Image.

Kitchen-table Goth girl critics.

Is this really the world I've always dreamed of?

"On second thought, the odds of ever impressing your haters are nil, so you should probably go for it. If you play it right, you can retire by the time you're eighteen, then none of it will even matter, right?"

"Retire at eighteen? And then what?"

That's only five years away—and the way he says it, like I'm sure to be washed up by then, well, it feels like a bullet speeding straight toward me.

"I don't know, what do all the other has-beens do? Go to rehab, wait for their chance to appear on *Where Are They Now?*, sit on their shrink's couch, and cry about what could've been?" He laughs.

"One Christmas duet—*one*—and you're already pegging me as a has-been?"

Dougall shifts in his seat and leans toward me like a doctor about to diagnose a serious illness with no cure. "I hate to break it to you, bro, but you were destined to be a has-been from the day you started this journey."

The way he says it, the way he looks at me, I can't help

but wonder if he somehow knows this is all a weird dream. Maybe he's in on it too.

But when he says, "Name one teen sensation from the past that managed to stay relevant," I know he's just making a point.

It's not like I rack my brain. I haven't lived long enough to know that many people. Still, I can't think of a single one.

"My point exactly." Dougall grins, clearly overcome with the satisfaction of being right. "So why not just accept the inevitable and enjoy the ride while it lasts?"

SWOOSH

By the time I've gotten used to the taste of coffee, I no longer hate it, my cup is empty, my brain is thrumming, my body is vibrating like it received a megadose of adrenaline, and I'm still in the limo, still in the dream.

The only difference is, I no longer care.

Dougall is right.

I need to sit back and enjoy the ride while it lasts.

I mean, jeez. Here I am, an International Superstar wielding some seriously solid bank (as Dougall would say), and all I can do is try to return to a place where I'm a Brainiac Nerd with $132.59 (thanks to Nana's annual Christmas/birthday checks and accumulated interest) to my name.

It doesn't make sense.

Not to mention, the more I hang with this new version of Dougall, the more I like him.

For one thing, he's nothing like the Greentree Dougall. He's like a billion, trillion, gazillion times cooler.

For another, he apparently has loads of celebrity contacts. Well, I guess technically they're my celebrity contacts, but Dougall knows what to do with them.

Also, he knows how to have fun. Real fun. Not the kind that's relegated to eating Cheetos and watching old Roswell documentaries on a couch covered in cat hair. We've been hanging out for a while now, and I haven't heard a single mention of Bigfoot, black holes, or conspiracy theories. The Greentree Dougall would never last this long without mentioning one of those things.

According to Dougall, who's pretty much an authority on celebrity life, it's way too early to show up at Jonah's party (only a dork gets there within three hours of the start time), so we decide to head out for some burgers to soak up the caffeine.

Sparks is pretty good at eluding the paparazzi, which isn't easy when you're driving a limo. And yet, even though we arrive without a bunch of photogs snapping my picture, even though Sparks went in first to scope out the restaurant and consult with the manager on securing the very best seat, the second we enter, the place erupts into chaos, with everyone snapping pics of me on their cell phones as the manager whisks us to a private booth in the back.

Sparks insists on guarding our table and plants himself

right at the edge. His back ruler straight, feet planted wide, his head swivels back and forth, like he's scoping for would-be assassins. It's kind of cool to have my own personal badass on call, but it still really bugs me to have him hanging around and eavesdropping on our conversations. So I order him to take a walk, grab a bite, maybe even read a few chapters of *Lord of the Flies*—a joke that admittedly falls kinda flat, but that's only because he doesn't know that in Greentree he assigned that book to our class.

At first he's reluctant to leave, but after I toss him a handful of bills and basically tell him to scram, he gets the hint. And as I watch him walk away, I gotta say, it feels pretty good to tell a teacher what to do for a change.

The second he's gone, our booth is invaded by girls practically crawling all over me as they grab at my T-shirt and run their hands over my hair, which for some reason makes them squeal, all the while telling me how much they love me, how they cry nonstop when they listen to my music, how they have pictures of me posted all over the walls of their rooms and inside their lockers at school. They ask me to sign their napkins and T-shirts. There are even a few requests to sign random body parts (mostly arms, legs, and hands, except for one forehead, which seemed a little strange).

At first it's really fun. I mean, what's the point of being an International Superstar if you can't enjoy a little time with your fans? And it's not like Dougall is left out, since they take pictures with him too (only with a little less enthusiasm).

But it's not long before it seems like every single one of

those girls texted every single person in their contacts list, because the next thing I know, the place is slammed with fans and photogs—none of them ordering food, which annoys the manager and the waitstaff so much I end up having to ask Sparks to return so he can escort us back to the limo, which is where we end up eating our burgers.

"This is so much better," Dougall says. "It's not like you can recline and put your feet up in a restaurant." He leans his head back against the seat, gazes up at the roof, and chews thoughtfully.

"Maybe I should open a restaurant," I say, the words garbled from a mouth stuffed full of fries. "One where instead of booths we have recliners, and instead of tables we have trays that slide out of the armrest, and instead of facing each other we'll all be facing these individual screens where we can watch whatever we want, 'cause it's all on demand." I laugh like I'm joking, but really I'm not. It seems like a truly inspired idea that might actually work. Besides, what's the point of having all this money if I don't have fun with it and build cool places for my friends and me to hang out?

"Dude—that's genius!" Dougall takes a long, loud sip of his soda, making a series of obnoxious slurping sounds as he scrapes the straw along the bottom. "You can call it The Den. But it won't have any signs. And it'll have a secret entrance and a secret phone number too. It'll be the hottest place in town—people will be fighting to book a recliner! You'll be even richer than you are now!"

I wipe a glob of ketchup from my chin and nod. Not

really getting the whole no-sign, secret-entrance-and-phone-number bit—I mean, how are people supposed to find it? Still, I've already decided to make some phone calls first thing tomorrow and get this idea going.

I'm kind of surprised by how easy it is to get used to being rich. I always figured it might require some time to adjust. But here I am, only a few hours in, and I'm already starting a business. And really, why stop there? What's the point of having a big fat wallet if you're not going to empty it? So I slide open the divider and tell Sparks to take us to the nearest Ferrari dealer.

Dougall swears it won't matter that we're not old enough to drive. He says once they see us—me in particular—they'll close off the showroom to all the sad wannabes and give us the run of the place.

"They'll probably even toss in a bunch of free logoed stuff too. You know, like hats and T-shirts and coffee mugs," he says. "Since anytime you step out in it, you'll be advertising for them."

It sounds good to me. In fact, it sounds pretty dang close to perfect. Which is why it's so disappointing when we arrive, only to discover that it's closed.

Since we can't test-drive Ferraris, we decide to do the next best thing: we tell Sparks to take us to a mall that has an Apple store, a Nike store, and a GameStop, which is something you'd never find back in Greentree, since you have to drive three towns over just to get to a mall, and even then, it only has one of those stores. But here in Tinsel Hills, it exists. And it's so amazing I don't even know how to explain it, other than to say it's three stories of awesome, with just about every store you could ever think of, all of them decorated for Christmas. There's even a ginormous Christmas tree that starts on the first floor and reaches all the way to the third and has thousands of ornaments hanging from it. And when I see the Santa's Village they've set up, well, I can't help but stare.

Back when I was a little kid, the place where my mom used to take Holly and me for our annual picture with Santa always reminded me of a red-and-green foil-wrapped bus stop that wasn't nearly as festive as it tried to be. But here it's a truly authentic village with a forest of fake pine trees covered in snow and a small log house where Santa waits for his elves to bring him kids to sit on his lap and tell him their wishes.

"You should do it," Dougall says when he catches me staring.

"What? No!" I'm embarrassed he caught me.

"Seriously, bro, a picture like that would make your Twitter and Instagram accounts explode! Your fans will go crazy—you'll break the record for most retweets, guaranteed."

I try to drag Dougall away and head for the Apple store so I can get a new phone, telling him there's no way I'm sitting on Santa's lap, but he's determined to convince me.

"Who said anything about sitting on his lap?" Dougall screws up his face. "You do the manly thing and stand side by side. Tell him you were named after him. That should make him happy."

"Since when does Santa need me to make him happy? Being jolly is pretty much his full-time gig."

"Maybe so, bro." Dougall laughs. "But it's still good PR all around. Not to mention how the mall executives will knock themselves out trying to find a way to return the favor, especially if you include them in the hashtag."

Despite the convincing argument he makes, the potential for extreme embarrassment is dangerously high.

Then again, Dougall really does seem to know what he's talking about when it comes to this stuff.

The next thing I know, I'm flanked by overexcited elves marching me past a stream of crying kids and annoyed moms toward Santa, who tells me he's one of my biggest fans as we drape an arm around each other's shoulders and smile brightly for a cell phone pic. Once that's done, Dougall and I head to the Apple store, where I buy a new phone along with all kinds of stuff I probably already own, but hey, it's always good to have backups.

Dougall loads up too, and I just put it all on my credit card. After all, that's what rich friends are for.

But when we move on to the Nike store, I stop dead in my tracks.

"Is that—"

My hand lifts and my index finger unfolds, seemingly guided by a force all its own.

"Is that . . . *for real*?"

I point toward a scene so insanely epic I can't think of a single word to describe it.

Because there—right there in front of us—spanning the entire floor-to-ceiling window space—is a giant picture of me, performing before a sold-out stadium of screaming fans.

And directly in front of that is a Christmas tree built entirely of white sneakers with metallic red and green swooshes and holographic gold stars, and the best part is—those kicks are named after me.

The sign reads:

Dashaways!
The Christmas Countdown begins with a limited edition—
available only for the next 5 Days!

While the Mojo endorsement seemed pretty cool—this—*this!*—is a whole other level that can only be described as Extreme Epicness.

I can't stop staring.

I'm on the verge of hyperventilating.

"Yeah, they're cool." Dougall shrugs, not nearly as impressed as he should be, even going so far as to shoot me a look, like I'm overreacting, as though he sees this kind of thing all the time. And maybe he does, but I certainly don't. He pushes his hand against my back and steers me inside. "It's pretty genius of Ezer to tie it into your show and song and all."

"We should buy some!" I say. "We'll get a pair for everyone we know."

I'm about to go in search of a salesperson when Dougall pulls me back. "Dude, I already have three pairs. And you have about a hundred. I don't see the point of paying for things you get paid to wear. Why don't we buy some other cool stuff instead?"

I stall. Despite what he says, I still think it qualifies as monumental to actually buy a pair of sneakers named after myself.

It's not like Josh Frost ever had sneakers named after him.

But once everyone in the store starts to recognize me, the moment is lost. And while Dougall is free to pick out a bunch of cool stuff for himself, I spend the next hour signing boxes of recently purchased shoes until the pyramid is dismantled, the shoppers are all leaving with at least five boxes each, and the store is completely sold out.

When we leave, we're escorted by a team of mall-appointed security—all of them talking sideways into their headsets, ensuring our privacy and safety, while pushing carts full of our newly acquired belongings. Even so, every girl who sees me starts crying and screaming and begging me to pose for a gazillion cell phone pics.

"And that is why we usually opt for your personal stylist to do the shopping for us," Dougall says as we climb into the back of the limo and the security team loads our shopping bags into the trunk.

I have a personal stylist?

No wonder I look so good in my pictures.

But what I say is "Yeah, but sometimes it's good to be out in the world. You know, be with the people. They get so excited when they see me, I feel like I'm giving them ..." I want to say *hope*, but that's not it.

"You're giving 'em a whiff of Dashaway magic," Dougall says. "A brush with true star power and greatness."

It would be a really great statement if he didn't ruin it by laughing the second after he said it.

"Anyway, bro—speaking of greatness, what do you say we head over to Jonah's party and see if the girls really did honor the luau theme?"

I'm a little miffed by the laughing, but ultimately I decide to let it go. After all, it must be hard for Dougall to hang out with me sometimes, with everyone always screaming my name and not his. I just hope no one at the party asks for my autograph. My hands are maxed out for the night.

HULA GIRLS

"What about us?" I ask. "Are we expected to honor the theme?" We're on our way to Jonah's party, and I'm getting kind of nervous. Dealing with fans is one thing—they're pretty much thrilled with whatever you do. But dealing with celebrities is a whole lot trickier. Or at least I imagine it is—it's not like I know from experience.

"No worries. It's handled." Dougall reaches into a bag by his feet, only to unearth the two most hideous Hawaiian shirts I've ever seen. One red, one blue, but both of them covered with similar images of hula girls, flowers, surfboards, rainbows, and dolphins wearing sunglasses. "I picked 'em up while you were signing at the Nike store. And don't worry, they're supposed to be ugly—it's kind of the point. We're being ironic."

I button the shirt over the T-shirt I'm already wearing so that if Dougall's wrong and it turns out to be not ironic at all but mortally embarrassing, I'll be able to whip it right off and pretend it never happened.

"Figured we didn't want to go overboard with the theme, since it's better to think of this as the starter party. You never know where it might lead."

We've barely climbed out of the limo when I motion toward a pretty girl wearing a grass skirt and pink bikini top just a few feet away. "Dude, is that—" I start to say, but before I can finish, Dougall is yanking on my sleeve and pulling me toward the limo.

"Change of plans." He gestures frantically at Sparks, whistling loudly for him to return. Kind of like you would for a dog, which makes me feel embarrassed for all of us. "Trust me," he says. "You definitely do *not* want to go there." He glances over his shoulder and shoots me a serious look that has me more curious than concerned. "You need to steer clear. Ever since you dumped her for her now-former best friend, she's been gunning for you. Just because you have selective amnesia doesn't mean she does."

As hard as it is to imagine a world where that could be true, apparently Dougall is right. The second she sees me, her eyes go all squinty and her mouth gets pinched, and after whispering something to the girl beside her, she marches straight toward me just as Dougall opens the limo door and shoves me inside.

"Thanks for having my back." I peer through the tinted window, disappointed to find she's given up the chase and settled for scowling instead. I was hoping to experience what it's like to be the perpetrator of a big romantic drama—or any drama involving an angry girl who isn't my sister.

"That's what I'm here for." Dougall settles in beside me. "Think of me as your best bro-slash-social director."

I stare at him, more than a little stunned by his words. That's exactly the kind of friend I've always wanted—exactly the kind of friend I wanted the Greentree Dougall to be. Someone who truly understands the value of popularity and exactly what it takes to maintain it.

"So what do we do now?" I peer through the back window, watching as crowds of people head for the house, sorry to be missing out on my first big celebrity bash. Though it's probably best to let Dougall take the lead. He seems to know his way around these things so much better than me.

"Whatever we want." He sprawls along the bench seat. "Sky's the limit. Seriously, when was the last time anyone said no to the 'Dashing Nick Dashaway,' as the tabloids call you?"

"Um, how about a few hours ago, when Plum Bailey said I was a sellout?"

At the mere mention of her name, Dougall's face softens. "Yeah, well, that's the great thing about Plum. She's special.

She's not like the other girls who hang around your house. For one thing, she doesn't even like hanging around your house. For another, she's impossible to impress. That's what I love about her. She's so . . ."

While Dougall's busy singing Plum's (apparently numerous) praises, Sparks brakes for a handful of girls who look like supermodels—the kind you see wearing angel's wings in Victoria's Secret commercials—heading straight for the limo.

"Nick, you in there?" One of them taps on the glass and peers inside.

I look to Dougall, unsure what to do. I narrowly escaped one angry ex, and for all I know she could be another. When he nods his approval, I lower the window.

"I thought I recognized your ride. Not many limos out there with your name on the license plate."

She fixes her gaze on mine as she smiles shyly. Well, maybe not *shyly*. She really doesn't seem all that shy. *Flirtatiously* is probably a better word. I'm just not used to using those descriptions in relation to myself.

"That is one seriously ugly shirt. Then again, if anyone can pull it off, it's you." She flips her blond hair over her shoulder the way I've seen Tinsley do countless times for Mac Turtledove, and all I can do is sit there and gulp as I try not to stare at her tiny grass skirt and coconut shells.

"Are you leaving already?" one of the brunettes asks. She's wearing an outfit that's pretty much an exact replica of the blond girl's, only her grass skirt is shorter.

"That party's lame." Dougall's tone is so disdainful it makes me feel bad. I mean, we never actually made it inside, so there's no way to be sure. "I wouldn't risk it if I were you."

The brunette checks with her friends before returning to us. "Do you know of any better ones?" Her gaze settles on mine.

"There's always a better party." Dougall grins. "And if there isn't, we'll start one—right, bro?" He bumps his fist against my shoulder a little harder than necessary, then gives me a look that says our future happiness pretty much depends on my going along.

I take a deep inhale and meet her gaze just like Josh Frost would, only better, because in this world Josh Frost doesn't exist. I've taken his place. "Plenty of room."

I prop the door open and slide across the seat, watching as they all pile in. Figuring that since there are no consequences in dreams, I might as well play along and see where this leads.

19

PINHEAD

At my suggestion, we end up at a bowling alley, and not a single person complains.

It's not even one of those cool, modern, loud-music-and-black-lights rock 'n' bowl kind of places either. It's a normal, standard-issue bowling alley, which is just how I like it. Though the surprising thing is everyone else pretends to like it too.

Then again, why wouldn't they? It's like Dougall said: no one says *no* to the Dashing Nick Dashaway.

All I have to do is declare bowling cool, and it is.

Sparks escorts us inside, and it's a good thing too, because the second all the other bowlers see me, his bodyguard skills are the only thing that keeps me from being trampled to death. Luckily, it's not long before the manager ushers us into his office for safekeeping while he clears the crowd and closes the place to the public. Exactly the kind of perfect solution that never would've occurred to me, even though it seems really obvious once it's done. I mean, while it's nice having fans and all, there's really no point in being famous if you don't take advantage of the kinds of perks that allow for a little privacy and peace.

When I offer to pay for the inconvenience, he's quick to brush it away. "Just take a pic with me and post it on Twitter," he says. "And make sure to hashtag the name of the bowling alley. That's all the compensation I need." Then he throws an arm around me, and we each break into a grin as Dougall takes the pic. It's seriously that easy. He even offers the girls a bunch of logo T-shirts to wear in case they get cold bowling in coconut shells and grass skirts. Though while they're all quick to take one, not a single one of them changes.

After we swap our regular shoes for bowling shoes and I help everyone choose a ball, we divvy up into two teams of three, and Blonde #1 volunteers to go first. (I know it probably sounds bad to call her that, but I've already forgotten their names, and I'm too embarrassed to ask.) She cradles the ball at the center of her chest (a typical amateur move) and awkwardly trots toward the foul line with her fingers practically death-gripping the ball. By the time she releases it, her swing is so off, the ball makes the world's slowest journey down the lane. A total creeper if I've ever seen one.

I have to admit, it's kind of funny to watch. Especially

the way her face goes all sad and droopy when the ball flops into the gutter well before it gets anywhere near the pins. I mean, she looks like she's truly surprised, like she actually expected an entirely different outcome. Which only makes it funnier.

Dougall immediately swoops in to hug her. A move that's meant to seem like a show of support, even though he's clearly taking advantage of the moment to hug a pretty girl.

At first I'm annoyed by the way he's always scheming to get what he wants, but when she pushes Dougall away and comes at me with arms spread wide, saying, "Hey, Nick—can I get a hug from you too?" well, it makes me sad that Dougall always has to angle for the things that come so easily to me.

Before she can reach me, Blonde #2 plops onto my lap, circles her arms around my neck, and says, "Back off, Tiffany. He's all mine." Then she kisses me smack in the center of my cheek, leaving a sticky lip-gloss tattoo as if to prove that it's true.

The redhead (I think her name might be Kayla, but it's not like I'm willing to risk saying it out loud in case I'm mistaken) laughs and snaps a pic of Blonde #2 and me; then, when Blonde #1 slithers up to my side and the redhead moves in beside her, Dougall joins in and snaps a bunch of group selfies that he instantly posts.

It's funny to think how I spent most of last year complaining about being invisible to girls, and yet now that I have four superhot girls practically fighting over me, I'm annoyed by the way they keep plucking at my hair and my clothes and telling me over and over again how cute they think I am.

Maybe it's just that I'm not used to having girls pay me so much attention (other than Plum, but like I said, Plum doesn't count). All I know for sure is that it leaves me feeling awkward and weird. It's not normal behavior. Or at least, it's not normal where I'm concerned.

I disentangle myself and head for the ball rack, determined to impress them with a skill I can actually claim in my Greentree life too. Even though I know this is all just a dream and I should try to enjoy whatever attention I get however I get it, I can't help wanting them to admire me for who I really am, as opposed to who they think I am.

Thing is, I'm a good bowler. And by good, I mean really, really good. I've been bowling since I was a little kid and was considered one of the best in my league. I've even got the trophies to prove it. Though it's not exactly something I'm used to advertising about myself.

Back in Greentree, Dougall and Plum are the only kids at school who know about my mad bowling skills. Mainly because none of the popular kids would be the least bit impressed. All they seem to care about is sports involving smaller, lighter balls, like football, basketball, and baseball. Not a single one of them would appreciate the fact that, in the world of bowling, I'm what's known as an anchor. Which means I'm the one who always bowls last so I can anchor the score. But tonight I decide to shake things up and go next.

Only, as soon as I'm standing at my start line, ball poised

and ready, I'm overcome by this horrible urge to faint, hurl, or both, which pretty much makes it impossible to move.

They're all looking at me, waiting to see what I'll do. But here in this strange dreamworld I have no way of knowing if I can still pull this off.

I tell myself it doesn't matter. That even if I totally blow it and end up with a gutter ball, they'll still act as though I did something brilliant. That's just how it is when you're famous. No one ever tells you like it is. But for once in my life, even if it's just my dream life, I want to know what it's like to have a beautiful girl, or in this case several beautiful girls, cheer for me in a way I deserve.

"Come on, Nick—you can do it!" the brunette shouts.

"You got this!" Tiffany cheers.

Dougall looks on with the same kind of skeptical face the Greentree Dougall made right before I took the stage in that unfortunate talent show.

I take a steadying breath and center my focus. I've got a lot riding on this moment, no matter how silly it seems.

Determined to prove my worth and prove both Dougalls wrong, I take four and a half slightly shaky steps toward the foul line, then release the ball and watch as it tears down the aisle. Ultimately crashing into the center pin so hard it not only falls but takes all the other pins with it.

And as soon as the pins are reset, I do it again.

And again.

Blowing rack after rack and scoring so many strikes

the employees, including the manager, gather to watch. The girls jump up and down, shouting and cheering, and when Dougall joins in, well, it's just the sort of validation I need to reduce that fiasco of a talent show into nothing more than a distant, hazy memory.

DECEMBER 20
4 Days, 14 Hours, 32 Minutes,
and 24 Seconds
till Christmas

#LAME-O

Turns out, just because one is an International Superstar with serious bank, no parental guidance, and therefore no curfew does not mean he doesn't have to answer to a higher authority.

In my case, that higher authority is Ezer.

"What's this?" He looms over me, shaking his phone in my face.

I squint one eye open but only so I can locate the nearest spare pillow and pull it over my head until I can no longer see him. Still, his muffled words manage to penetrate.

"Great way to make use of your Twitter account!" Even

from under the pillow I can tell that the words are fueled by high-octane anger. "Using your 140 characters for this little gem: *Leaving Jonah K's lame-o luau!* Then, since you presumably had more characters to spare, you added the hashtag *WorstPartyEver.*" He pulls at the pillow and tries to remove it, but I just tighten my grip. "What the heck, Nick? You serious? Slamming another celebrity like that? What's gotten into you?"

The honest answer is, I don't know. Pieces of the night are just now starting to assemble in my brain—something about my phone being passed around so the girls could take selfies and . . . and send them out into the world.

At the time, it seemed like the best idea ever. The girls were enjoying it. Dougall thought it was hilarious. And when I sent that tweet about Jonah, didn't everyone laugh so hard we practically fell off our seats?

"Meanwhile," Ezer continues, adopting an overly dramatic tone, "over on Instagram, there's a charming pic of you and Dougall with a bunch of half-naked girls who are old enough to babysit the both of you. What the heck were you thinking?"

"They weren't half-naked," I mumble. "They were wearing grass skirts and coconut shells—the party was luau themed . . ."

"What? I can't hear you, Nick. Speak a little louder, please." Ezer wrenches the pillow from my head, and I don't try to fight him.

Images of the night are stampeding through my brain.

So much stuff it seems impossible to fit all of that into one single night.

But according to Twitter, Instagram, and Ezer, we did.

"They kept all their clothes on the whole entire time, I swear."

"Sure, but that's only because they were barely wearing any to begin with!"

He's glaring at me. I can feel it. But as of now, I can't bring myself to look at him.

"And they weren't nearly as old as you claim. Sixteen at most."

"Sixteen, really? You sure? You check their IDs, Nick? Because in a town where thirty-year-olds are regularly cast to play teens on TV, that really means a lot."

"What's your problem, anyway?" I sit up so abruptly I forget my bed is not only round but set smack in the middle of my room, which means I nearly fall off the edge. And while I may recover quickly, don't think he didn't notice. "Sheesh, would you just relax? *Nothing* happened. We took some pictures, drove around for a bit, bowled a few rounds, what's the big deal?" I climb out of bed, about to go into my closet to get dressed, when I see that I already am. Seems I slept in my clothes, and they don't smell so good.

They smell like cigarettes—like secondhand smoke, which is what it must be, since I would never do something so stupid as smoke. It's disgusting. Besides, I distinctly remember signing an antismoking pledge in sixth-grade health class.

"Nothing happened? You sure, Nick? Maybe you should take a look at your Twitter account, where you live-tweeted your night."

I start to reach for the phone, wanting to get to the bottom of who's responsible for making my T-shirt smell so bad, when Ezer yanks it away before I can reach it.

"And if that wasn't enough, the entire pictorial was also posted to your Instagram, Tumblr, and Facebook accounts." He shakes his head, takes a deep breath, but the truth is, he looks like he's about to implode. "What did I tell you about social media, Nick?" He pauses as though I'm seriously supposed to reply. "I said that it's great for self-promotion—until it's not. Until you lose control and decide to document your break with reality, which is exactly what you did here."

"Okay, whatever. So I made a mistake. What are they gonna do, fire me?"

I roll my eyes and start to head for my bathroom, stopping dead in my tracks when he says, "No, Nick, no one's going to fire you. They'll just stop buying your CDs and watching your show. Oh, and as soon as your sales and ratings plummet, your endorsement deals will dry up. And then, in order to continue living your luxurious lifestyle, you'll be expected to *actually pay for it*. But with your money stream gone, you won't be able to afford it. And while you can ride it out for a few months, it won't be long before the bank seizes your homes, your cars, all the stuff you hold dear. Your staff will be out of work, because you can't afford to pay them. And your family will be out on the street, since you'll lose the homes you bought for them too. But hey, that's okay, you can all shack up together again in the same three-bedroom, two-and-a-half-bath that you all started in, with nothing left but the memory of your wild night on the town with your supposed friend Dougall and a group of grown women who were only using you to promote themselves."

"You're blaming Dougall?"

"Is that all you got out of that? Dougall is a problem. A very real problem. The worst kind of hanger-on. He's riding your coattails. He's nothing without you, and don't think he doesn't know it. But at the moment he's only a blip on your list, because let me tell you something: that scenario I described is all too real. It happens all the time. There's no inoculation for failure, especially the kind we bring on ourselves."

I shake my head. It's not like I didn't hear, 'cause I did. I just don't get why I'm still here.

Why I haven't woken up already and found myself back in Greentree, frozen solid on the bus stop bench.

How I can let so many people down, including myself, when dreams have no consequences?

"And if you still don't believe me, if you're still delusional enough to think you can just float through your life because no one would dare question the Dashing Nick Dashaway— tell me this: Exactly how are you going to sell your bad behavior to your twelve-year-old fans who are madly in love with you? And, more important, how are you going to sell it to the parents of those twelve-year-old girls who supply the weekly allowance that enables those girls to spend it all on

Nick Dashaway crap? Huh, Nick? Tell me, how you gonna do that?"

"Um, plead temporary insanity due to an overdose of caffeine and a surplus of supermodels?" I try to crack a joke, but it fails miserably.

"You want to pretend you're Hugh Hefner, find another fan base!"

"Who?" I squint, and even though the question was sincere, it only serves to infuriate Ezer.

He grumbles under his breath and tosses me the phone so I can get a firsthand look at my wild night, which looks way wilder in pictures than I remember it being. The only moment I can clearly grasp is how excited I felt after bowling six strikes in a row. The rest is a blur.

"Oh, and for the record, those bowlers you kicked out so you could have the place to yourself—"

I return the phone and frown. "What—you mean my fans? They were practically mobbing me. Besides, it was the manager's call, not mine."

"Yeah? Well, it looks like they've had a change of heart. Didn't appreciate getting kicked out in the middle of their games, and they've taken to the Internet to vent their outrage. Some serious damage control is in order, Nick. I want you in the studio with Tinsley every day, working on a squeaky-clean Christmas love song that'll—fingers crossed—make everyone forget about the night of Nick Gone Wild. And when you're not in the studio, I want you lying low. No showing your face at the Starbucks drive-thru in pursuit of free coffee. No dropping into burger joints and sending Sparks away."

"How did you know about that?" I ask. I didn't even have my new phone at that point.

"I know everything, Nick." His expression turns to one of extreme wariness, like all of that anger has morphed into worry.

And since I can't stand for anyone to be disappointed in me, I do my best to convince him it wasn't nearly as bad as he thinks. "It really wasn't that big a deal," I say. "Behind the pictures, it was mostly all talk. Everyone does that back in Greentree. You know, trying to look way cooler than they are." The moment it's out, I realize I never should've mentioned Greentree, but since it's too late to take it back, I can only hope Ezer doesn't call me on it.

"I don't know what or where that is, but you're already cool," Ezer says. "Now you need to learn how to live up to the responsibility that comes with it." Even though he's starting to sound like my dad, like he only has my best interests at heart, he's been yelling at me for so long it's hard to make the transition.

"What's the point of being an International Superstar if I can't live my own life?"

Ezer turns to me, eyes gleaming, lips curving, as though he's been waiting for me to ask exactly that.

"The point is to sell records and whatever else you can get your name on before the tide turns, you age out, and someone cuter, younger, and, most important, *newer* comes along. You want to live your own life? You can either go back to being an invisible nobody or wait until you're washed up, which, at this rate, shouldn't take long. You're no indie rocker, Nick. You're a squeaky-clean teen dream. You need to start acting like one. Now get yourself together and meet me downstairs. I'll delete the pics from your account and deal with any immediate fallout. Tinsley's already at the studio, waiting for you to show up."

"Did Tinsley see the pics?" I ask, really hoping she didn't.

But Ezer doesn't reply, so I do as he says and head for the shower.

UNEXPLAINABLE PHENOMENON

So far, the strangest part of today is the fact that I'm still here.

Still in this life.

Still in this house.

Still getting yelled at by Ezer for being myself.

Clearly this is no dream.

Clearly I'm not slowly freezing to death back in Greentree.

I'd be long dead by now if that was the case.

Which leads me to my next theory.

I've seen enough documentaries with the Greentree

Dougall about string theory, M theory, vibrating strings, alternate dimensions, time warps, black holes, mysterious portals, and other kinds of unexplainable phenomena to know that weird stuff just might really exist. And while I may not fully understand all of it, I've always found it fascinating.

Still, it's one thing to be fascinated by a concept—it's another to find yourself living in one of them.

How else am I to explain how I went from being a Brainiac Nerd to ending up here, in this bizarre otherland where I'm the most famous teen in the world?

I mean, one minute I'm approaching death by hypothermia, and the next some insane Christmas trolley is hauling me off to Tinsel Hills . . . and . . .

And . . .

And . . . when that crazy driver asked me where I wanted to go, I said, *"To a different, better, much cooler life."*

And that's when Plum's candle blew out.

Plum!

She brought all this about!

She gave me that dumb birthday cupcake with its stupid candle that, even though I don't understand it, served as some kind of portal that landed me here.

And didn't she practically *force* me to make a wish?

Didn't she say something really pushy, like *"And choose your wish carefully—sometimes they really do come true!"*

Which means the wish—not the candle—was the portal.

Only, the candle made the wish possible.

Whatever. One thing's for sure: Plum set this in motion. She conjured up the conditions that brought me into this world.

Question is—why would she do that?

Is it so I could find myself in a place where the tables are turned and she thinks I'm the biggest dork/loser/sellout?

If it's revenge she's after, then I'm afraid it's going to backfire.

Why would I give a flying flip about Plum when I've been ordered to spend the next week in a recording studio with Tinsley Barnes as part of my punishment?

And if I really am in an alternate dimension, and what that trolley driver said was true, then I have four days left to enjoy this life to the fullest before the return ticket expires.

One minute past midnight.

Christmas Day.

My dream deadline.

I head into the closet to confirm that the ticket is still stashed in the pocket of the hoodie I arrived in. Catching a glimpse of myself in the mirror, I realize what a fool I was to drink so much caffeine in an attempt to go back.

I've been acting so dumb I can hardly believe it.

Seriously. Talk about some major bonehead activity.

I mean, wasn't my image as a Brainiac Nerd a full-time job back in Greentree?

At least here I have an image worth keeping.

Not to mention how worked up I got after seeing Tinsley

with Mac Turtledove, acting as though I couldn't possibly compete, which, in retrospect, is hilarious.

Just because Mac is still taller than me—has bigger muscles than me—is better looking than me—doesn't mean he can compete with my International Superstar status.

Tinsley deserves someone better than Mac.

Someone like me.

Besides, what exactly would I return to?

A life as an invisible nobody, where Tinsley Barnes literally walks right over me without slowing down?

A mean, bratty sister and completely stressed-out parents worried about back taxes and year-end financials?

Why would I ever want to return to that when I can stay right here in Tinsel Hills and live out my life as the hottest, most celebrated star in the world with the kind of family and friends I've always dreamed of having? I mean, it may take some doing to get used to the new version of Sir Dasher Dashaway, but with Holly acting so nice and my parents so happy and relaxed and letting me do whatever I want, it's definitely worth the trade-off.

I've got four days to decide, but really, the choice is already made.

I zip the pocket shut and make my way downstairs, where Plum's mom, Lisa, catches me on my way out the door, trying to hand me a glass filled with something that looks like green slime.

"Ezer said you're not feeling well. I thought this might help."

I eyeball it suspiciously, making no move to take it.

"It's a—hangover cure." She shifts uncomfortably when she says it. Like she's embarrassed for me that it's come to this.

"I'm not hungover." I wave it away. "Never felt better!" I add, directing the words to where Plum watches me from behind the cover of a book that looks as serious, dark, and boring as she is.

For a second I consider pumping her for some info— seeing what she might know about the cupcake, the wish, and how I ended up here. But then I think: *Who even cares?* I'm here. It's awesome. And I have no plans to go back to my former life as an invisible loser. Also, I'm positive our conversation would be just as painful as our last one, and I'm definitely not up for that this morning.

Once I'm settled in the limo, Tinsley texts me a photo of her insanely beautiful self, grinning as she holds two red Starbucks cups in her hands.

They won't stay hot forever. Better hurry! she writes, completely unaware of the irony behind her words.

I won't stay hot forever.

Tinsley won't wait forever.

I need to hurry.

Still, I take it as a sign that I'm on the right track, tell Sparks to make it quick, then slam the divider shut and sprawl across my seat, feet propped on the window, as I stare at the picture of Tinsley until the limo pulls up to the curb.

NAUGHTY OR NICE

22

COOL LIKE THAT

Just as I'd always suspected, it's absolutely, one hundred percent true that girls really do like bad boys. Guys who seem a little unpredictable at times. Maybe even a little rough around the edges.

I went straight from Ezer's meltdown regarding my wild night on the town with Dougall to the studio where Tinsley was waiting with my red Christmas-themed Starbucks cup, and it was obvious there'd been a power shift. I reached for my drink without bothering to confirm it was mine. And from the way she'd looked at me, well, I was clearly in the driver's seat.

She sat on a stool, legs crossed at the knees, and waved her cell phone at me. "Surprised you even showed up after a night like that." Her voice was a little sharp and high-pitched, but I didn't respond.

I took my time sipping my Peppermint Mocha, which, by the way, is the number one trick to having power. Not the sipping the Peppermint Mocha part but the making her wait part. The thing about power is, you have to own it and use it in order not to lose it.

Then, when I was good and ready, I looked at her and said, "I thought Ezer deleted all that."

Her lips pressed together as her eyes appraised me in a whole new way. "He can't delete my screen shots." She frowned at her shoes while I did a little fist-pumping victory dance in my head.

Tinsley Barnes took a screen shot of me!

It was all I needed to hear.

I looked around the studio and shrugged, like it was no big thing. "We should probably get started. I've got a slew of interviews and a photo shoot lined up after this, and then of course we're shooting the show tonight."

She cleared her throat, brushed a hand through her glorious hair. "Ready when you are." And it's been nothing but sweet, sweet music ever since.

Except when it wasn't.

The first couple of takes were awful.

Then we gradually went from truly awful to just plain bad. Until somewhere near the end of the session, we'd reached a point where we didn't feel like covering our ears and screaming in order to drown ourselves out, which is pretty much when Ezer arrived, listened to a few sets, and told us to call it a day and meet back tomorrow, same time and place.

Which brings me to today.

Not only did we sing the song the entire way through without a single flub, but there was no mention or sign of Mac Turtledove, which probably means Tinsley is committed to moving on to bigger and better things—namely, me.

It also marks the first day since I arrived that we're not filming a new episode of the *Twelve Days of Dashaway Christmas Countdown*, since Ezer says they have enough footage to piece something together and everyone deserves a night off.

All of which is reason enough to celebrate. Which is why I'm throwing a party.

It's all part of the plan to take my relationship with Tinsley to the next level. Tonight's the night I'm going to kiss her.

Despite all the time we spend in the studio and Tinsley's increasing appearances on my show, where she's mostly required to laugh at my jokes and look really cute, we're never alone long enough for me to show her how I feel about her. Ezer is always right there, which makes it impossible to so much as hold her hand when his beady eyes are always watching us like the world's most annoying chaperone.

Well, tonight's the night when all of that changes.

When Tinsley sees what I have planned, there's no way she'll be able to resist me.

We're just wrapping up for the day, both of us gathering

our stuff, when I casually say, "Oh, hey, I think I might've mentioned I'm having a little get-together tonight. If you're not busy, you should stop by."

Tinsley looks at me sideways, turning away as she mumbles, "From what I heard, it's hardly a get-together."

She's right about that. It's about as far from a get-together as one can possibly get. I put my entire team to work on planning, organizing, and making sure everything's perfect. It's costing me some serious bank too. But if it earns the kind of rewards I'm after, it'll be money well spent.

Still, I just shrug and say, "Feel free to swing by around eight." Thereby following the number two rule of playing it cool, which is to not look too excited about anything, ever. Better to just sit back and assume all good things are coming to you. Which is exactly why celebrities rarely smile in selfies—they know it's far better to look bored than excited.

But when she doesn't reply or even acknowledge that she heard me, I realize for the very first time that she might actually choose *not* to come by.

Which would defeat the whole purpose of throwing an elaborate party.

Which makes me break out in an immediate sweat.

"Mmm, I don't know, Nick." She tosses her bag over her shoulder. "Ezer wants us back here bright and early, and you know how he gets when we're overtired or late or, God forbid, both." She exits the studio and opts to take the stairs instead of waiting for the elevator, which, granted, is known to be slow, but still, the way she races down the steps, the soles of her sandals making loud clacking sounds, makes me wonder if she's trying to ditch me, which only increases the sweating.

I'm right on her heels. The thud of my sneakers slamming the stairs sounds as hollow and desperate as I currently feel. "Just because Ezer was born middle-aged doesn't mean we have to act that way too." I try not to sound winded and panicky but don't really succeed. "Bring him along if it makes you feel better," I add, instantly wishing I hadn't. "I'd hate for you to miss it, Tins—it's gonna be epic."

She reaches the ground floor, pauses before the smudgy glass entry door, and pulls her lips in, like she's sneaking a taste of her vanilla lip gloss while she considers her options.

"Heck, bring Ezer *and* a friend—the more the merrier!" I cry, having made the full transition from panicked to pathetic. "What's your boyfriend's name again?" I arrange my face to look like I'm struggling to remember, even though I'm unlikely to ever forget the name that's haunted me since my Gymboree days.

She squints. Tilts her head to the side. "You mean Mac?"

I hold my breath, waiting to see what comes next. Will she confirm they're still together? Make a face and laugh, telling me she and Turtledove are officially over?

The seconds tick past.

The silence drags.

"Well ... maybe ... ," she finally says. "I have some stuff

to do at home ... and I'm not sure Ezer will want to go, so I'll need someone to drive me...." She places her palm on the door and gives it a shove.

"I'll send the limo!" I speak the words so quickly, it's clear to both of us I've just willingly forfeited every last trace of cool. "Believe me, Sparks won't mind." I cross my arm over hers as though I'm trying to do the polite thing by getting to the door first, when mostly I'm trying to close this deal before she can get in Ezer's waiting car, start texting Mac, and forget I exist.

"You'd do that?" She studies me, her face so close I can make out every individual eyelash, every single blue fleck in her irises, and yet it's impossible to read what she's thinking.

"Sure," I say. "Why not?" Hardly able to believe I just offered Tinsley and Mac the use of my limo.

She continues to stare, all the while doing this twisty thing with her lips. "Mmm, okay ... ," she finally agrees, which isn't exactly the enthusiastic response I was after.

"Great, it starts at eight." I leave her with that, not wanting to drag this out any further and give her a chance to change her mind. I head for the limo, where Sparks holds back a crush of the exact same fans who wait in the exact same spot every day on the off chance I might profess my undying love and marry one of them.

All the while I'm replaying the conversation in my head and arriving at the startling conclusion that I've been fooling myself all along.

Tinsley's been in charge the whole time.

OPERATION MISTLETOE

By 8:35 the music is blaring, my house is packed wall-to-wall with people, and yet all I can do is pace before the front windows, so focused on Tinsley's arrival I can't even enjoy my own party.

"Dude, what gives?" Dougall comes up from behind me and shoves a red plastic cup into my hand. "You are missing some truly epic events going down by the pool."

I take a sip from the cup, then spit it right back.

"What's the problem, bro? It's just Mojo—your drink of choice." He laughs. "I may have doctored yours up a bit, but that's only to help you relax. You're gonna burn a hole in that carpet if you don't put the brakes on."

I return the cup, more than a little annoyed with my

friend. The last thing I need is to kiss Tinsley with messed-up-Mojo breath. Dougall knows just how important this night is. Heck, I pretty much let him plan it. Since I've been spending so much time with Tinsley in the recording studio, I thought it'd be good for him to have something to do other than bug me while I'm trying to work.

Dougall ditches the cup on a side table and turns back to me. "Uh, I hate to break it to you, but this party was *your* idea, remember? Not that anyone actually needs you to have fun, but people kind of like seeing the host bangin' it up now and then."

"Yeah, well . . ." The words fade. I can no longer remember what I was going to say.

Sparks just pulled up in the limo.

He's slipping out of his side of the car and going around to open the door.

And when Tinsley climbs out, I hold my breath, waiting to see if Mac's with her.

I turn to Dougall, grab him by the shoulders, and shake him so hard his own cup of Mojo spills all over my floor, but I don't even care.

"Dude, what the heck?" Dougall peels my hands off his shoulders and squints out the window, but Tinsley's already on her way to the door, so there's nothing to see.

"Nothing. Never mind. Just—" I glance around, hardly believing it's all turning out just as I'd planned. Tinsley came to the party alone. Clearly she's over Mac Turtledove. "Who's the hottest girl at this party?" I ask.

"You mean besides Plum?" Dougall tosses his now empty cup on the table next to mine.

I roll my eyes. "Yeah. Whatever. Other than Plum, who's the hottest girl here—or even the second hottest? I need you to take me to her, like pronto. Tinsley's about to walk through the door!"

★

It may seem like a jerk move, to stand by a window pining for a girl to appear, only to ignore her the second she walks through the door. But I couldn't risk scaring her off by showing what a nervous, sweaty mess I was at the thought of her not showing up.

So by the time Tinsley finds her way out back, I'm deep in conversation with a group of very hot girls I've never seen before and will probably never see again, but there's no reason for Tinsley to know that.

"Such a great party!" they say. "Such a cool house!" And "Omigod, I *so* loved that episode where you and Holly got in that Christmas cookie fight—hilarious!"

They grin in this really fake way, as though they're peering at me through a veil of spotlights and dollar signs, and all I can think is how Tinsley never looks at me like that. Like I'm the quickest way for her to move up in the world.

Sure, I'm helping build her career by recording the duet together and letting her be on my show, but Tinsley likes me for me. I have no doubt it's true. I mean, while I'm still not sure if she sees me as a potential boyfriend (though tonight I intend to find out), I can say with absolute certainty that she's one of the few people since I got here, other than my family and Ezer, who treat me like a normal person and never suck up to me.

Tinsley's always really sweet, that's just how she is. But she never does anything false, like laugh at one of my jokes unless she truly finds it funny. Dougall does that all the time, and it's starting to get on my nerves. Sometimes I wish he'd act more real, more like the Greentree Dougall. Which probably sounds weird, considering how much I wanted the Greentree Dougall to act like the one here.

I know it seems like a petty complaint, but when you're an International Superstar with practically everyone applauding everything you do, it makes it nearly impossible to tell who's being sincere and who's not.

When I see her wandering around with a red cup in her hand, I'm quick to ditch the girls and edge up beside her. "If you got that from Dougall, you might want to think twice about drinking it." My voice is cool, my expression even cooler. "He's kind of a bad influence."

"Are you talking about Dougall or you?" Tinsley tosses her drink in the nearest can as I make a face, pretending to be deeply offended by the question.

"Don't believe everything you read," I tell her. "Deep down I'm an angel."

"Really?" She tilts her head to the side, causing her hair to spill over her shoulder in soft, golden waves. And in that moment her beauty is so mesmerizing I have to remind myself to breathe.

"Someday, if you're lucky, I'll show you my halo," I manage to reply. Feeling proud of myself for delivering the line with such a cool, bad-boy edge. Especially considering how nervous I am.

It's pretty much the kind of line that'd make any girl fall madly in love with me on the spot. Which is why I don't understand when Tinsley's only response is to laugh in a way that seems really forced as she shifts her attention toward a group of kids playing some diving game in the pool.

I fall silent beside her, not entirely comfortable with how that went down and unsure how to proceed. Then again, it's possible I misread the whole thing. She's probably just overwhelmed by all the excitement, which is perfectly understandable, considering how this is the kind of party you only see in movies. And while it may not have a theme, like Jonah's party, that's only because my party is of such epic proportions it's impossible to pin down.

There are waiters walking around with large trays of food—and not the weird, boring, bite-sized food adults serve at parties, but real food. Good food. Like sliders, mini pizzas, little cups stuffed with French fries—the kind of food you *want* to eat. There's an ice cream sundae station attached to a caramel and chocolate fountain that you can drink from, and a DJ by the pool spinning really good music, a lot of it mine. There's even a bunch of random photo booths where you can choose your own background, which, going by the long lines, seems like a hit.

All around me are hundreds of people I don't even know. Some of them famous like me.

But no one's as famous *as* me.

And that's exactly what I remind myself when I look at Tinsley and say, "Did you bring a suit?" I nod toward the pool, where her eyes are already focused. Plenty of people are floating around the lazy river and lounging on the fake beach. "It's heated. Last I checked, it was hovering around ninety degrees." When she shakes her head, I do my best to cover my disappointment. I've barely had any time to get in that pool, and I was really hoping to do so with her. "Yeah, I hear ya," I say. "Seems kind of weird to be swimming so close to Christmas."

"Does it?" She crinkles her nose and studies me carefully.

"Well, yeah. Back in Gr—" I start to say *Back in Greentree,* but luckily I catch myself and go straight into recovery mode. "Well, you know, in movies, Christmas always takes place somewhere snowy and cold."

"I wish I could see that." Her eyes go soft and dreamy, and her breath does this sort of faint wistful sigh. "You know, a white Christmas? I've lived here my entire life, and we've never once gotten close."

Finally. Up until now I've been walking on a tightrope, but this I've got covered.

"Better stick around, then," I say. "Sometimes wishes come true."

★

By ten o'clock, just like I'd planned, a heavy layer of snow starts to fall in my backyard, courtesy of the professional snowmakers I rented.

At first it takes everyone a moment to realize what's happening, but when the crew dressed as Santa's elves bring out the inner tubes, and the waiters wearing Santa hats circle the crowd with heaping trays of hot chocolate and snowman accessories like carrots, black hats, red scarves, and glossy black pebbles to use for the eyes, well, that's when the real fun begins. Everyone starts making snow angels, having snowball fights, and taking snow-covered selfies. People will be talking about this party long after they've forgotten about all the others.

Luckily, also as planned, Tinsley and I are standing directly under the mistletoe I've hung from a palm tree. The moment I've been waiting for is finally here.

"Oh, Nick!" Tinsley thrusts her arms wide as she spins under great swirls of snow that drift onto her cheeks, making her look like some kind of irresistible winter fairy. "I can't believe you arranged this! It's just—magic!" She settles before me with glittering eyes and a face so radiant I can no longer resist.

I inch closer, point clumsily at the mistletoe hanging above. "Oh, look at that," I say, as though the moment hasn't been carefully choreographed. Watching in stunned amazement as her face softens and her lips push apart, like she knows what's coming and fully intends to kiss me right back. Like she wouldn't even consider screaming and running away.

"Nick . . ." She moves toward me, the tips of her fingers finding my arm. "Nick?" she repeats, but the moment was lost the second I spotted the cameraman lurking off to the side.

24

I KNEW YOU WERE TROUBLE

"Seriously?" I pace the rug in my den as soon as all the guests have cleared out, which started just after I spotted the cameraman and then Ezer and well before the fireworks show could begin. "You seriously filmed my party? Is nothing sacred to you?"

"Sacred?" Ezer laughs. "Tell me, Nick—what exactly is it you hold sacred?" He leans his head back against the cushion and peers down the length of his nose.

"My privacy, for starters! You invaded my space without my permission! You invaded my private moment . . . not to mention my . . . privacy!"

Okay, so maybe that was a little repetitive. It's hard for

me to speak clearly when I'm flustered like this. Not to mention, I didn't even know he was here. I mean, even my family knew better than to come, and my invitation to them was sincere!

"Your privacy?" Ezer balks. "Allow me to remind you, Nick, that as per our agreement, I have every right to film your party. Not to mention how you happily gave up any semblance of privacy the day you signed on to become a celebrity with your own reality show. Back when you were living life as an invisible nobody, you had plenty of privacy, and if you'll remember correctly, you longed for the opposite. You couldn't wait to hit the big time—and now that you have, you're complaining about that. You can't have it both ways, Nick. I gotta be honest here, you are seriously testing my patience."

The way he sighs, closes his eyes, and rubs one of his meaty hands across his face, well, I'm worried that he might try to fire me for being such a pain, and then I won't have access to Tinsley.

But the feeling lasts only a few seconds before I remember I'm Ezer's only client.

He can't afford to fire me.

I'm in control, and I need to start acting like it.

"No more, Ezer. No more backyard ambushes. No more secret filming without my consent—which would mean it's not exactly secret, so yeah, no more secret filming, like I just said." I continue to fidget and pace, wishing I was better at expressing myself, especially at moments like this.

"I think you'll feel differently when you see the final edits." He inspects his fingernails, acting as though he hasn't bothered to listen to a single word I just said.

"Doubtful." I stand before him, arms folded across my chest in an attempt to appear bigger, more authoritative, though he doesn't seem to notice.

"I hear we got some nice footage of you and Tinsley. Wouldn't you like to relive that look on her face when the snow started falling? I assume that was the whole point of the snow machines—all of it, really. Tell me, Nick, am I wrong to think you organized the whole show for Tinsley?"

I do my best to hold my own and maintain eye contact with Ezer. But everything he just said makes me feel ashamed and transparent. It's like he has X-ray vision and can see right through me. Good thing Sparks drove Tinsley home. I'd hate for her to witness this mess.

"Tomorrow, Nick." Ezer pushes off the couch and slaps a heavy hand on my shoulder, but I'm quick to duck from his reach, so his arm ends up falling loose to his side. He doesn't react, doesn't even seem to notice. He just heads for the door, saying, "Ten a.m. sharp. Don't be late." Like always, he gets the last word.

As soon as he's gone, I sink onto my couch, surrounded by a giant mess that'll stay that way until the cleaning crew arrives in the morning: overturned cups dripping Mojo onto just about every available surface, a broken lamp, turned-up rugs, rearranged furniture ... I don't know how famous people throw parties like this on a regular basis. It's really destructive.

"For what it's worth, I thought you handled that well." At the sound of Plum's voice, my heart practically leaps from my chest. I had no idea she was here. And I definitely didn't invite her.

I turn to find her awkwardly folded into the acrylic bubble chair that hangs from the ceiling by a thick silver chain, heels resting on top of her knees like some kind of yoga pretzel, with an open book on her lap resting on top of a folded Santa hat. It seems like she has spent the better part of the night exactly like that.

Still, it's not like I'm interested in her input, even if it is positive. Knowing this Tinsel Hills Plum, she's just trying to soften me up so the insult that follows will have greater impact.

"Where's Dougall?" I ask, sure he's to blame for inviting her.

She shrugs and makes a face. "How should I know? Up until an hour ago, I was helping my mom."

Time to hire a new personal chef. One who doesn't come with an annoying daughter who insists on hanging around for the sole purpose of judging me.

"Ezer had no right to film you without your knowing. I mean, I don't remember signing a waiver, do you?" She does that thing where one eyebrow goes up and the other stays put. "The second I spotted that camera, I was outta there. Which is kind of a shame, since I missed the part when it started to snow."

I sink my head into my hands. "I'm pretty sure I signed

my life over to Ezer the first day we met." When my eyes dare to meet hers, I'm surprised to find she's not wearing her usual hypercritical expression. She seems sincere. Maybe even concerned. Completely free of hidden agendas and ulterior motives. Like she's somehow morphed into the opposite version of everything I've learned about her, reminding me of the Greentree Plum.

We sit like that for a while, no words passing between us other than the ones that come from our eyes. Then she untangles herself, shoves off the chair, and says, "Even with the cameras, as far as parties go, this one was epic." She tucks her hair behind her ear, but the curls, just like in Greentree, spring right back in place. "Though I'm not sure you should have to go to all that trouble just to get a girl to kiss you."

I close my eyes and groan. Apparently I'm so transparent even Plum saw right through me.

"It doesn't have to be so complicated, Nick." She pauses, waiting for me to acknowledge her words. "It doesn't have to be some big grand thing. If she wants it to happen, you'll know by the look in her eyes, the way she lingers in your space." She slips her bag onto her shoulder, preparing to leave, but as strange as it seems, I can't let her go. If she has a deeper perspective into these things, then I need her to share it with me so I can stop messing everything up.

"What do you know about it?" I say. Only it comes out sounding defensive and wrong, when what I really wanted to ask was what she knows about Tinsley's willingness to kiss me—since she's apparently so good at reading people.

179

"Well, for starters, I *am* a girl." She folds her arms across her chest and juts one hip to the side. So sure of herself and the subject it makes me wonder who she might've kissed. Possibly someone like the skinny rocker dude she seemed so obsessed with in the magazine?

The thought leaves me deflated.

I'll never understand what girls are really thinking.

Or why they do the things they do.

Say the things they say.

Like the people they like.

They're pretty much the biggest mystery in the universe.

"She wanted to kiss me," I say. I'm not sure why, but I feel the need to explain. I can't let her leave thinking I'm pathetic and delusional. "It was right there in her eyes—just like you said."

"Well, okay, then." Plum lifts her shoulders and drops them back down, as though it's decided. But it's not. Not even close.

"But then I saw the camera and . . ." My voice fades, no point in going on.

"You know what your problem is, Nick?" Her fingers pick at her sleeve as her mouth curves into a grin, as though she can hardly wait to lay it on me.

I shoot her a wary look. As far as she's concerned, the list of my problems is infinite, and I'm not sure I'm up for hearing it. Still, I feel like I should beat her to the punch, let her know she can't get to me no matter how hard she might try.

"That I'm a soft sellout who makes manufactured, inauthentic crap I try to disguise as music?" Repeating pretty much the exact same things she told Dougall.

"No, not that." She waves it away, doesn't even try to deny it. "You're a romantic, Nick Dashaway. That's your real problem. And this town is brutal for people like you."

She looks at me for a long moment, peering through thick layers of mascara and black eyeliner like she wants to make sure her words have really penetrated.

Satisfied, she makes for the door. And that's when I realize how much I want her to stay.

But that's probably only because I don't want to be alone.

I've barely had any time to myself, and I guess I've gotten so used to being surrounded by celebrities, fans, and employees of the Nick Dashaway show that I forgot how nice it is to be treated like a normal person.

I'm about to call her back, but I'm a few seconds too late.

"Night, Nick," she says, almost like it's an afterthought. Her dark hair swinging over her shoulder, she places the Santa hat on the entry table and leaves me in this big, empty house, all alone with my thoughts.

25

DECEMBER 22
2 Days, 7 Hours, 32 Minutes,
and 43 Seconds
till Christmas

GUESS WHO'S COMING TO DINNER

By the third take, we've nailed it.

Or at least, that's what Ezer claims.

If it were up to me, I'd opt to go again, but he insists it's all there.

"If anything's missing, we'll fix it in the edit," he says.

"But I don't want it to come off as overdone," I tell him, surprised to find I'm only three days in and I'm already growing tired of the signature Nick Dashaway manufactured sound. "I want it raw, kind of earthy and gritty. Maybe we should try an acoustic version, just to see?"

Ezer looks at me like I'm crazy. "You're a star, not an artist. Be happy for that. It means you're not starving for attention, money, or anything else."

I start to object, but Tinsley cuts me off. "I'm with Nick." She shoots me a covert look, like we're in this together. "It would be fun to try, and it might sound even better on the show. You know, make it seem more spontaneous, less rehearsed."

"Yeah," I say, encouraged by Tinsley's argument. "We could put some chairs next to a Christmas tree, and Tinsley could play guitar, and I—"

"I like it." Ezer nods and squints into the distance, like he's watching the whole scene unspool on the far wall. "It could work." The nod grows more convinced.

"Of course, we'll need a tree," I say. Which, now that I think about it, is a really strange thing to be missing, considering we've been filming the *Christmas Countdown* since the day I arrived. My house is still only partially decorated.

"It's handled. Everything's handled," Ezer says. "Though I do like Tinsley's idea. Tell you what, you two get your acoustic version worked out, and if it's any good, we'll include it in the tree-trimming episode. Good thinking, Tins."

He gives her shoulder a squeeze and leads us outside, and I try not to be overly miffed by how the whole thing went down. If Ezer wants to give Tinsley credit for something that was clearly my idea, so be it. As long as it happens, it doesn't really matter who gets the acknowledgment.

"Hey, I just thought of something." Ezer stands before the elevator doors, rubbing his hands together in the way he does when he's dreaming about large, gleaming piles of money. "The second the episode airs, we'll make the songs available for purchase. We'll see if we can swing an exclusive with iTunes—I'm sure they'll be thrilled to have it. Heck, we'll give 'em both the studio version and the acoustic version so we can watch 'em duke it out for number one. Either way you'll score the number one and number two spots on the charts!"

It's a good plan, there's no denying it. Still, I find it funny how he acts like it's all for my benefit, like he doesn't get a hefty chunk of the cut. Maybe I've never been to his house, but my guess is, he's living large.

"How come you never invite me over to your house?" I shield my eyes from the sun as I follow him and Tinsley outside. "How come you're always at my house and I'm never at yours?"

"You want to come over?" Ezer pauses before his big black Escalade.

I nod, my gaze never once veering from his. I want to see where he lives. Maybe get a peek at Tinsley's room. Any excuse to be near her and hopefully finish the moment I started at the party.

"Well, all right, then. Why don't you stop by for dinner tonight?"

I hold his gaze, not sure I trust that it's really that easy.

But when I switch to Tinsley and see her smile excitedly, that's when I realize just how paranoid working with Ezer has made me.

"Great," I say. "See you at seven."

★

Just as I figured, Ezer is living the good life.

His house is big. Sprawling. Like a castle, with lots of stone and big turrets. The only things missing are a drawbridge and a moat filled with alligators.

First thing I do when the maid answers the door and leads me inside is check for cameras.

Did I mention how paranoid he's made me?

If there's one thing I know for sure, it's that Ezer wouldn't dream of missing a filmable moment for the *Twelve Days of Dashaway Christmas Countdown,* but for tonight anyway we seem to be clear.

Guess he values his own privacy more than mine.

The maid directs me to the den, where Tinsley sits on the couch near the fireplace, strumming her guitar and singing softly, as though she hasn't just spent the entire day doing just that, while Ezer barks into his cell phone from somewhere in the next room.

"Nick—hey, I'll just be a sec." He butts his head in, fixes a hand over the speaker as he whisper-yells, "Why don't you two practice a bit?" Then, before we can answer, he's back to yelling into his phone.

Tinsley slides over, making room for me. She starts from the beginning as I clear my throat, wait a few beats, then pick up on cue. She looks so pretty in her blue dress, with her hair falling in soft waves around her face, it's all I can do to keep my focus on singing. With our voices blending so well, I'm kind of lost in the music when Ezer appears before us, claps his hands loudly, and says, "That's it. That's exactly what I'm looking for. Now, if you can just duplicate that at the studio tomorrow, we'll be swimming in platinum!"

I close my eyes and groan. I'm so sick of the studio. While it's nice having access to Tinsley for hours on end, it's mostly spent working. Not to mention that there's no way I'll ever get to kiss her in that boring, sterile room that's always crowded with Ezer and sound geeks.

"But that's enough shop talk for today," he says. "Let's get you two fed. You're going to need plenty of energy for tomorrow." He herds us into a dining room that fits right in with the modern castle theme, with its supersized table, big iron candelabras running down the center, heavy wood chairs with legs carved like claws, and so many heaping platters of food it's hard to take them in all at once. When Ezer takes his place at the head, lowering himself onto a large velvet cushion, the only thing missing is a crown.

Even though I kind of make fun of him and his castle house in my head, I have to admit, the food is really good and the conversation's not nearly as boring as I expected. Maybe it's the luxury of actually sitting down to a meal as opposed to always eating on the run, maybe it's the goblet of wine in Ezer's hand—whatever the cause, pretty much for the first time ever, Ezer loosens up and actually talks about stuff that has nothing to do with untapped endorsement possibilities, the show's ratings, or the number of units "Twelve Days" has sold on iTunes.

It's so nice hanging out like this, almost like we're a family, that I find myself wishing I could stretch each moment just a little bit longer so the night would never have to end. It also makes me determined to spend more time with my actual family, since the only time I ever get to see them is when we're filming the show, and even then every moment is micromanaged and scripted. Once, when I complained to Ezer, he claimed he had no choice but to keep us apart. *They'll just get in the way,* he said, which doesn't make any sense. From what little time I've spent with them, they seem really nice and supportive, always willing to pitch in and help. Holly included, which is not something I could ever say about the Greentree Holly.

I'm beginning to think Ezer has major control issues.

When the dessert course is presented, I'm about to dig in, but then Ezer and Tinsley both decline theirs, so I decline mine as well. And the next thing I know, the plates are being cleared, Ezer is back to yelling into his cell phone, and that warm family feeling is gone.

Tinsley leads me into the den, and the moment we're alone, she does a spot-on impersonation of Ezer that gets me laughing so hard I'm practically wheezing. But when we settle onto the couch and she tells me how Ezer isn't technically her uncle—how her parents died when she was a baby, and Ezer, her dad's best friend, stepped in to raise her, well, suddenly it's not so easy to laugh at him anymore.

It's pretty much the last thing I expected. I guess because it's a surprisingly nice and decent thing to do, and I didn't expect that of Ezer.

"In the early years he raised me all on his own." She leans back against the cushions and crosses one leg over the other as her gaze blurs into memory. "He couldn't afford a nanny until I was around eight and he started managing a boy band that shot straight to the top. When the money started pouring in, the first thing he did was buy this house and hire someone to look after me. I wouldn't have any of this if it wasn't for him."

The second I hear that, I can't help but feel guilty for mentally accusing him of being a control freak when all along he's just been doing his best to protect me.

"When the band broke up, he planned to take an extended vacation, maybe even walk away from it all." She rubs her lips together and looks right at me. "But then he heard you sing, and he figured the vacation could wait."

I lean in, eager to hear more while also trying to pretend like I've heard this story before, like I actually lived it.

"He said you were rough around the edges but it wasn't anything that good training couldn't fix."

Her lips curve into a smile, and she looks so pretty I'm

forced to turn my attention to the glass of Mojo the maid just placed before me.

How could I have gotten it so wrong? All this time I've been annoyed with Ezer, thinking he was the bad guy, always getting in my way and telling me what to do, when in reality it's not like that at all.

"Said you reminded him of himself when he was your age."

Hunh?

I guess I was so engrossed in my thoughts, I lost track of what Tinsley was saying. But that got my attention, mostly because it's exactly what Josh Frost said.

"Ezer used to sing?" As much as I try to picture it, it's impossible to imagine. It's easier to see him as one of those WWE wrestlers than as a teen heartthrob.

"No, silly. I'd have thought you would've known that."

She pushes me playfully on the shoulder, and her hand lingers a few seconds longer than necessary. But I'm so busy trying to think of something to say to cover the flub I forget to enjoy the feel of Tinsley's touch. And just when I start to, her hand returns to her lap.

"He meant you're both ambitious, driven to succeed. Ezer tried to sing, but it didn't take long to realize he just didn't have it—you know, that thing that makes someone worth watching?"

She tilts her head to the side and scrunches her nose the tiniest bit, but no matter how irresistible she may look, I can't help thinking: *Yeah, that* thing. *That indefinable thing I didn't have in Greentree but I surely do here, even though I'm exactly the same.*

"Anyway, it's cute how he thinks of you as his son."

I wait for the punch line, sure that she's joking. From the way Ezer's always lecturing me, I figured he thought of me as his biggest annoyance. But when she leaves it at that, I say, "Are you serious?"

"Well, yeah." She settles deeper into the cushions, crosses her legs at the knee, as though it's as simple and obvious as she clearly thinks. "You know, especially 'cause your parents are kind of flaky and all. He thinks it's his job to look after you."

"They're not," I say, feeling suddenly defensive.

Tinsley looks at me, her fingers fidgety, face cautious.

"They're not flaky, they're just—" My voice fades; my argument deflates. Tinsley doesn't even know my parents. And how could she when all of their interactions are scripted? Heck, I barely know them myself.

"I'm sorry, I didn't mean ..." She places a hand on my arm and shoots me a look of apology.

"It's okay." I lean into her touch. "I mean, maybe you're right ... you know, about them being flaky and all. After all, they're hardly ever around. ..."

It's not fair what I'm saying, and not entirely true. But with the fireplace blazing, soft music lilting, and Tinsley's face just inches from mine, looking like she might actually intend to kiss me, well, words don't seem to matter.

Seems Plum was right—it doesn't have to be some big, grand thing.

When a girl wants you to kiss her, you'll know from the look in her eyes, the way she lingers in your space.

I rub my lips together, feeling bad that they're a little chapped but determined to make the best of this. I close my eyes the way they do in the movies, about to make the big move, when Ezer barges into the room.

"Party's over, you two. I need you in the studio bright and early."

DECEMBER 23
1 Day, 16 Hours, 21 Minutes,
and 16 Seconds
till Christmas

DO YOU HEAR WHAT I HEAR?

They say it takes twenty-one days to build a habit, but I've been in Tinsel Hills for less than a week and already every day is starting to look like a repeat.

The first thing I do after getting my 7 a.m. wakeup call is grab the schedule Plum's mom slides under my door, which usually goes something like this:

8 a.m. Breakfast in the limo.
9 a.m. Meet Tinsley at the recording studio.

1 p.m.–1:15 p.m. Lunch break at the studio.

5 p.m. Return home to shoot the *Twelve Days of Dashaway Christmas Countdown*.

6 p.m. Dinner (squeeze in between hair, wardrobe, and makeup or during filming).

12 a.m. Fall exhausted (and somewhat frustrated) into bed.

Okay, maybe I added that last part. And it's not like I'm complaining or anything, since I had a pretty strict routine back in Greentree too, only it wasn't nearly as exciting. Still, all that time spent recording and filming doesn't allow for much else. I mean, it's not like I'm trying to nitpick, but with the trolley ticket expiring tomorrow night at one minute past midnight, I need to commit to either staying here in my dream life or heading back home.

I thought I'd made my decision my second day here. I was sure I'd stay put and never look back. But there's one small thing that's been nagging at me—keeping my dream life from being as perfect as I want it to be (aside from my still not kissing Tinsley), and today's the day I do something about that.

I guess having dinner with Ezer last night made me realize how much I miss hanging with my family. Don't get me wrong—I like how they stay out of my way and never try to exert their authority by imposing stupid curfews and random rules, like most parents do (though Ezer has that covered). But since they're pretty much the family I always dreamed of having, I can't help but think it might be nice to spend a little more time with them.

Which is why today, instead of pretending to drink one of Lisa's totally disgusting but supposedly healthy smoothies for breakfast, only to make Sparks go through the Starbucks drive-thru on the way to the recording studio so I can get something decent, I'm going to have breakfast with my family. And we're going to hang out and enjoy the kind of real, spontaneous, unscripted conversations I used to have with my Greentree family. Only better.

★

I can hear them all talking in the entryway below, so I pause at the top of the stairs, hoping to go unnoticed long enough to hear what they talk about when I'm not around. But the voices all overlap in a way that doesn't make sense, until I realize they're ignoring one another in favor of their cell phones.

Holly: "No, I have no idea what time we'll be done. That's really up to Nick, isn't it? All I can do is hope it doesn't take too long and try to get through it."

My mom: "Well, can he squeeze me in at eleven? Eleven-fifteen? Eleven-forty-five? No, I have another appointment at one. There has to be a way he can see me. I booked this over a month ago, and I need to look good for tonight!"

My dad: "No." Sigh. "Not today." Grunt. "I have no idea

how long this will take, which is why I can't commit to anything firm."

When I reach the landing, they all turn to stare, with their cell phones raised before their ears. Looking anxious, uncertain. Like me, they have their own schedules to keep.

Unlike me, they don't seem to resent theirs as much as I've begun to resent mine.

My dad's the first to speak. Wearing a tight smile that seems glued to his face, he slides his phone into the front pocket of his khakis and says, "Nick—what's this about?"

I shift my gaze to my mom. Her expression is an exact match for my dad's. And when I look over at Holly, well, she looks a lot like Sir Dasher Dashaway when he pokes his head out of her purse: widened eyes, tilted head.

All of them caught in a state of suspended animation, waiting for me to explain why I pulled them away from their busy lives just to eat pancakes with me.

"Sorry." I try to wave it away as though it was all a big misunderstanding, feeling embarrassed, deflated, to realize I was so wrong about them. Clearly they don't miss spending time with me. If anything, they'd prefer to avoid me. "I'm not sure what I was thinking. Or, more likely, wasn't thinking . . ."

I peek through a clump of hair that's fallen into my eyes. Wishing they'd stop me from apologizing, tell me I've got it all wrong—that they're happy to be here. My mom would give me a hug, my dad would give me a hearty slap on the back, Holly would jokingly call me a dork, then we'd all head into the kitchen and enjoy a leisurely family breakfast together.

Instead they continue to stand there, fidgety, twitchy, waiting for me to wrap this up so they can get on with their day.

"But I know you're all busy, so . . . I guess I'll see you at the live taping tonight." I nod, forcing myself to smile as I gesture for them to leave. Watching as they push through the door and rush toward their cars, in such a big hurry to get back to their lives they don't even think to say goodbye.

JUST LIKE IN THE MOVIES

Once again we hit it early on. But if there's one thing I've learned about this business, it's that if you want to be taken seriously, you have to pretend never to be satisfied, so I insist on doing it again.

Also, I'm reluctant to say goodbye to Tinsley.

Especially considering how every time Ezer leaves the room, Tinsley looks like she's relieved to finally have some time alone with me, even if the sound geeks are standing nearby.

But after another hour of redos, Ezer overrides me and calls it a wrap, claiming they have everything they need and that we should get some rest before tonight's taping, since we're broadcasting live.

"Are you nervous about tonight?" Tinsley asks as we make our way outside.

"Not at all," I say, not entirely sure what she's getting at. I mean, we tape a show almost every night. Why should this be any different. "Are you?"

"A little," she admits, though the look on her face tells me it's way worse than that. "There's no way to hide a mistake when it's live."

I guess I hadn't really thought of that. Still, it's not worth getting worked up about.

"I'm afraid of doing something stupid that'll end up going viral on YouTube. Especially since I've never had such a big part on your show."

I'm surprised to hear her say that, since it seems like she's always on set. But I guess by the time we're done with all the hair, makeup, and wardrobe prep, not to mention trying to act real while following a script, I have no interest in watching it play out on TV to see what Ezer did in the edits.

"Don't be nervous," I tell her, trying to sound reassuring, even though I've got my own private concerns.

There's only one day till Christmas.

One more day till my return ticket expires, along with any chance of returning to Greentree.

Even though I've decided to live out my life as an International Superstar here in Tinsel Hills, knowing I can never return to the old life is kind of a big deal. Especially after that botched family breakfast this morning.

"Guess that's the difference between an amateur and a

pro," says Tinsley, flashing me a sideways glance as her mouth droops into an adorable frown. "Every time the camera's on me, I feel like I'm about to throw up."

"I used to feel that way."

Her eyes narrow as though she's not sure she believes it.

"But then someone reminded me that the audience just wants to be entertained and inspired, and it was my job to give it to 'em."

A look of pure adoration washes over her face, like I'm some kind of god.

Which seems like as good a time as any to kiss her— except we're standing in the middle of the sidewalk just outside a recording studio, with Sparks watching over us from his place beside the limo.

"So what now?" I ask, motioning for Sparks to wait.

"Ezer wants us to take it easy so we'll be rested for tonight." She takes on this dutiful, good-girl tone, but her expression tells me she's up for something more exciting.

"Yeah, so where else could we do that—other than home?"

Her smile is sly. "What did you have in mind?"

"Well, I've never been to Disneyland," I say, remembering how the Pirates of the Caribbean ride has that one romantic spot with all the dim lights and fake fireflies. Or at least the one in Florida does.

"Seriously?" She seems shocked by the news.

"Yeah, I've been to Disney *World*," I say. "Not *Land*."

"So . . . you flew all the way to Florida to see a replica of what you could've seen just an hour down the freeway?"

I shrug like it's no big thing. Like that's just how I roll. Forgetting yet again she has no idea that I'm not really from here. Heck, most of the time I forget too.

She dismisses the idea with a wave of her hand. "If you've never been, you should really spend the whole day, because there's so much to do. How about we go to the beach instead?"

It's a brilliant idea. The weather is always so perfect; the beach in December is totally doable.

"It's actually my favorite time of year." She catches the end of her ponytail and twists it around in her fingers. "I like it better than summer. For one thing, it's not nearly as crowded, and, I don't know, I guess I feel kind of privileged to get to do things like that in the middle of winter when the majority of the country is knee-deep in snow."

"Then it's done." I lead her to the limo and tell Sparks to drive us to the best beach he can think of.

★

I thought the water would be warmer, like in Florida, but Tinsley just laughs and reminds me it's cold most of the year.

Cold or not, it doesn't stop me from kicking off my shoes, rolling up my jeans, and joining Tinsley at the place where the surf meets the sand.

"This is my happy place!" she says, nudging a shell with her toe, her face radiant in the fading rays of the sun.

"Mine too," I agree. Even though, other than a family

trip to Miami, where Holly and I took a single surf lesson, this is only my second time at the beach. But that doesn't make it any less true. With Tinsley beside me, I could be behind bars in a maximum-security prison and I would say the same thing.

The water splashes over our ankles and onto our shins as Tinsley lifts her skirt just past her knees and runs deeper into the waves, laughing and splashing and singing our song at the top of her lungs. It's pretty much the most beautiful sight I could ever imagine.

"Come on!" she calls. "What're you waiting for? Scared to get a little wet?"

And that's all it takes for me to hurl myself straight into an oncoming wave just to be near her.

"Much better." Her tone is teasing, eyes gleaming. "Except for your hair." She arcs her arm through the water, thoroughly drenching me in one single move.

So of course I splash back, and before you know it, we're in a full-scale water fight, both of us laughing so hard we nearly miss the oncoming wave.

But at the very last moment, I reach for her hand and pull her down with me. The two of us resurface simultaneously, wiping salt water and sand from our eyes, as my arm finds its way around her waist and she brushes my hair off my face. Her gaze soft and tender. Her lips parted. Looking so beautiful it's like she walked straight out of a movie.

Only if this were a movie, this is exactly the part where I would usually fast-forward until it was over.

But that was before I ever had a chance at the starring role.

I rub my lips together, hoping she won't find them too salty, then I take a deep breath and move in, fully aware of the miracle unfolding before me as Tinsley leans toward me with a look as eager as mine.

"Nick," Tinsley whispers, "promise me that no matter what happens, you'll remember this moment."

I have no idea what she means, but I don't waste much time thinking about it. How could I ever forget the day Tinsley Barnes decided it was a good idea to kiss me?

She snakes her hand around the back of my neck, her breath soft and sweet, the scent of sun and salt water and happiness wafting from her skin. Her lips are just millimeters from mine, so ready and willing, just about to touch down, when Sparks shouts at us from a few feet away.

I tune him out.

Whatever he wants can wait.

The moment I've been waiting for is finally here, and I'm committed to seeing it all the way through.

Unfortunately Tinsley doesn't share my commitment.

Which is how I end up with my lips lodged in her hair, somewhere north of her ear, as Sparks yells, "Ezer called. He wants you in hair and makeup now! They moved the taping up three hours."

YOU'RE A MEAN ONE,
MR. GRINCH

It's impossible to hide my annoyance with Ezer.

Especially after rushing all the way home only to find that the crew hadn't even arrived.

"What's the deal?" I barge into the den—*my* den—where Ezer sits on the couch, feet propped on the table.

He slips a hand over his phone and says, "In a minute, Nick." Then he takes his sweet time to finish the call as I pace around the room, dripping water everywhere. Tinsley starts checking the messages on her cell like she's used to standing in living rooms soaking wet while waiting on Ezer.

"You need something?" He finally decides to acknowledge us.

My mouth opens wide, but despite the speech I rehearsed in my head—beginning with a reminder of how he works for me—my tongue feels like lead and no words come out. With Tinsley standing beside me, glancing nervously between us, all I can manage is "Um, yeah. So we rushed to get here, but nothing's happening. What gives?"

He removes a pile of papers from his lap and sets them aside. Then, easing his reading glasses onto the tip of his nose, he studies me for a long, uncomfortable moment. "I told you to take it easy, to rest up for tonight, and you take that as permission to go frolicking about in a freezing-cold ocean."

I'm about to object to the use of the phrase *frolicking about,* but when I take a moment to think it over, it really does fit.

"And now here you are, soaking wet and shivering, at risk of losing your voices, all because you chose to do the exact opposite of what I instructed."

I mumble under my breath and roll my eyes like I've seen Holly (Greentree Holly) do a million times.

"Care to repeat that?" Ezer says as Tinsley shoots me a look full of worry.

"You're not my dad." I'm forced to clear my throat to get the words out, which only serves to prove his point.

"No, Nick, I'm not. But right now I'm the closest thing that you've got to one."

I don't know why, but at that moment my throat goes hot and tight while the backs of my eyes start to burn. I must be overtired. Or maybe it has something to do with this morning. Either way I need to get over it. I'm living the good life, the life of my dreams. So there's no reason for me to be feeling like I'm this close to doing something completely humiliating, like crying.

"Go take a hot shower, Nick." Ezer rises from the couch while I stand there trying to pull it together so I don't embarrass myself in front of Tinsley. "Get some rest. Tinsley and I will see you tonight."

Before I can reply, he's leading her out my front door.

KISS AND RUN

By the time I'm showered and dressed, my entire house has been transformed into a winter wonderland, with the Christmas decorations out in full force.

Every available surface is smothered in garlands, tinsel, wreaths, sprigs of holly, the works, and I can't help but think how much my Greentree mom would enjoy seeing this.

The cast and crew are gathered in the kitchen, everyone hoisting glasses filled with what looks like champagne but, knowing Ezer, is probably just sparkling cider.

"Just in time!" Ezer waves me over. "Grab a glass—we've got good news to celebrate."

I pinch my glass at the stem like I'm used to drinking out

of champagne flutes, then focus on Ezer. I have no idea what this is about, but I can feel his excitement from here.

"The show is a runaway hit!" he announces.

Everyone cheers, and while I cheer along too, I'm a little confused. Isn't that something we already knew?

"Filming every day was a risk that some at the network were hesitant to take. But I wouldn't give up, and it turns out I was right. The *Twelve Days of Dashaway Christmas Countdown* is seeing the highest numbers in the network's history!" His grin is broad, but it's probably more about being right than about the actual numbers. Most people love being right, but Ezer takes it to a whole new level.

Everyone turns to me, waiting for a response. So I lift my glass and say, "That's awesome!" which falls a little flatter than I would've liked, but it's not like anyone saw fit to write me a speech.

"Awesome indeed!" Ezer laughs, doing his best to cover for me. "In fact, it's so awesome, *The Lazy Daze of Dashaway Summer Sizzle* has gotten the green light! Though the title may change, so let's keep that under wraps until we have something final."

Everyone seems really excited by the news. Nothing like the thrill of working on a hit show. Not to mention the promise of a steady summer paycheck.

As for me, I'm busy picturing long, hot days spent on the beach next to a bikini-clad Tinsley. Surely I'll get to kiss her by then?

"So drink up," Ezer says. "We've got a record-breaking show to produce!"

Everyone drains his glass and clears out, leaving Plum and her mom to load up one of my two dishwashers. Ezer slides an arm around my shoulder and says, "There's something I want you to see." He leads me into the living room, where he gestures toward the towering Christmas tree that soars so high the tip nearly brushes against the two-story ceiling. "What do you think?" he says, studying me carefully.

The sight of it gets me so choked up I can't speak. Considering how Mac Turtledove's dad hijacked our Christmas tree back in Greentree, I'm pretty moved that Ezer went to the trouble to do this. How did he know just how much this would mean to me?

I guess Tinsley was right. He really does see me like a son. None of this would exist—the house, the limo, the tree, my reality show—if it weren't for him. I'm just an average kid with a mediocre voice and a really big dream, and Ezer managed to transform that into the world's biggest celebrity. The only reason he lectures me so much is because he wants the very best for me—including the very best tree.

"Yeah," I finally say, my throat clogged with emotion. "It's even better than the one at the mall. That one looked a little scrawny at the top."

Ezer laughs and slaps me on the shoulder in a way that seems really sincere as opposed to his usual pretending. And while I want to say more, want to let him know how grateful

I am for everything he's done on my behalf, my throat's so constricted I'm forced to rely on my face to say what I can't.

He pulls me in close, giving me an unexpected hug. Then, leaving me gawking at my tree, he moves away just as quickly, back to telling everyone what to do and say, even though he's not technically the director.

Typical Ezer. And yet it's the only way things get done around here.

You need vision to soar.

Besides, it's not my place to question his methods. Between me and the boy band he managed before me, his track record speaks for itself.

When I spot my parents and Holly just a few feet away, I make for their side of the room, determined to put the morning behind me and make a new start.

But before I can reach them, the cameras move into place, Christmas music swells in the background, and I've got no choice but to put the conversation on hold as we all move into our roles as a happy family about to decorate a giant tree. All of us are sipping hot cocoa from red and green mugs and sharing a good laugh when my own Christmas song slips into the mix and Sir Dasher Dashaway starts dancing on his hind legs and barking excitedly.

Tinsley arrives, arms loaded with gifts, and the others soon follow, mostly friends of the family I don't recognize, except for Dougall, of course. Still, with all of us together, well, even though we're filming, it really does make for a scene so cozy, so postcard perfect, it's easy to settle right in and pretend that it's real.

It's every picture you've seen of the ideal Christmas.

Or at least that's what I think until my mom claps her hands and says, "Time for presents!" and I realize I never took the time to go out and buy any. But apparently Ezer has my back once again, because when my mom starts handing out gifts, most are from me. And they're much better gifts than I would've found on my own.

When my mom opens a box containing the gold-and-diamond necklace I supposedly got her, she dabs the tears at the corners of her eyes and flashes me heart-fingers from her side of the room.

When my dad sees his shiny new golf clubs, he gives me a manly slap on the back and says something about the two of us hitting the course sometime soon.

Holly actually shrieks with joy when she opens her present to find the key to a new Vespa, hidden under a mound of red and green confetti that sprays all over the floor. Which is pretty much the polar opposite of last Christmas, when the Greentree Holly frowned at the gift card I got her and in her most sarcastic voice said, "Wow, thanks for putting a lot of thought and effort into my gift, Nick."

They seem so happy and grateful it makes me feel guilty for taking the credit when they should be thanking Ezer, not me. I've been so focused on trying to kiss Tinsley I'd practically forgotten they even exist.

After Dougall thanks me for the new Xbox I supposedly

got him, and I'm practically drowning in a pile of stuff my family bought me, Tinsley approaches from the far side of the room holding a slim, rectangular box in her hands, and I freeze when I realize there's nothing left under the tree that I can pretend came from me.

I clear my throat and stare at Ezer, willing him to acknowledge me, but he refuses to so much as look. Leaving me to wing it on my own as Tinsley sits beside me and thrusts the box toward my chest.

I balance the gift in my hands, examining it from all sides in a pathetic attempt to stall for time. Fully aware of the camera zooming in, knowing I'm just moments away from revealing myself as the most clueless guy in TV history.

"Merry Christmas, Nick." She grins excitedly, which only makes me feel guiltier.

"Um, thanks," I mumble, knowing that sounded even worse on film than it did in my head.

"Hurry up, silly," she says, watching me slip a hesitant finger along the edge of the ribbon. "I promise it won't bite or explode."

I tug on the ribbon until the whole thing unravels, then open the lid to find a single sheet of coffee-stained paper bearing the handwritten lyrics to my all-time favorite song, by my all-time favorite artist (aside from Josh Frost), signed at the bottom.

I'm speechless.

A gift like this isn't random.

It required some serious scouting and planning.

It required Tinsley to do some pretty intense research on me, since I don't remember ever mentioning it to her.

And suddenly, just like in Greentree, there's no denying that this girl is truly out of my league.

"Do you like it?" The tremor in her voice betrays her nervousness. "I read in one of your interviews, I think it might've been in *Teen Vogue,* that it was your favorite song, and I thought that maybe . . ." She mashes her lips together, as though she fears she's made a mistake.

"I love it." I force the words from my mouth. "I don't even know what to say."

What I want to say is *I failed you. I have nothing for you. I was so interested in trying to impress you and getting you to like me, mostly because you're so pretty, that I never really tried to get to know you well enough to know what you'd want.*

She blinks a few times. Heaves a dramatic, made-for-the-cameras sigh of relief. Though it's not long before a look of expectation washes over her face, and that's when my panic takes root.

I clear my throat again. Pathetic, I know. But how do you tell a girl who just gave you something amazing that you have nothing amazing to give in return?

And not only do you not have anything amazing in return, but you actually don't have anything at all?

I'm just about to admit to the horrible truth when I spy Ezer frantically gesturing to his jacket pocket. Which, after a few moments, I realize is meant to symbolize *my* jacket pocket. So I shove my hand inside, only to find that it's empty.

From across the room he continues the mime, practically pummeling his left side with his fist. And not knowing what else to do, I check my other pocket, and that's where I find a small white box bearing a shiny red ribbon that I absolutely did not put there. But that doesn't stop me from pushing it toward Tinsley and saying, "I think this is for you."

And yes, I really did say that: "I *think* this is for you." Like it's a mystery that needs to be solved. Which it is, but still.

Tinsley unwraps her gift like every bit is a work of art to be savored, taking the time to carefully fold the ribbon and place it on her lap before she lifts the lid, presses a hand to her heart, and squeals with delight.

Whatever it is, she seems to be thrilled, which is a giant relief.

Or at least that's what I think until I see inside the box and nearly hurl on the spot.

What the heck is Ezer thinking?

"Oh, Nick!" Tinsley squeals. "It's so beautiful—I don't know what to say. . . ."

That makes two of us, so I choose to say nothing.

And not just because the cameras are rolling in for a close-up, but because Tinsley Barnes is now looking at me in real life just like she does in my dreams.

Like I'm the most amazing boy she's ever seen.

When the camera zooms closer to better capture the moment and Tinsley slips the delicate gold-and-sapphire (same color as her eyes) ring onto her finger—not just any finger but her *wedding ring* finger—I feel like I just might pass out.

"When's the date?" my mom cries, clapping her hands as though it's pretty much the best news in the world when your son, who's still a day away from his thirteenth birthday, gets engaged to a girl the same age.

Tinsley laughs good-naturedly as she turns to my mom and says, "It's a *someday* ring, right, Nick?"

I smile weakly, the best I can do. I mean, I like Tinsley, I do. I've liked her every single day for the last year and a half without fail. But that doesn't mean I can promise to *someday* marry her. Heck, thanks to Ezer's constant interference, I still haven't even managed to kiss her.

And now he plants this ring on me?

What the heck is going on?

My parents and Holly act all excited, Dougall shoots me a thumbs-up that only seems sincere until you notice that his eyes tell a whole other story, Sir Dasher Dashaway dances in circles and barks like the well-trained purebred he is, and Tinsley grins so happily, admiring the way it glints on her finger, I feel like I'm the only one who's not enjoying the spectacle.

Until I catch a glimpse of Plum shaking her head and giving me a look that tells it like it is: I am the most played person she's ever seen.

But when my mom says, "Tinsley, did you check for an inscription?" she uses this giggly, girlish voice, like she's Tinsley's new BFF and not her potential, *someday* mother-in-law. "I always love when there's a hidden message inside."

Tinsley slips the ring off and reads, "'Someday I will make you mine. My love for you will never die.'"

She brings her fingers to her lips, apparently so moved she can't speak. But when her gaze meets my own, there's definitely something she's trying to hide.

She lowers her hand to her heart, and, feeding the camera her very best angle, she says, "They're lyrics to the new song we've been working on, 'Someday.'"

"I'd love to hear it!" Holly says. "Why don't you sing it for us?" She claps like she'd truly like nothing more as everyone else chimes in, in agreement.

"What do you think, Nick?" Tinsley asks as though she has no idea how I'll react.

And really, how could she?

Seems everyone else got one script while I got another.

Still, I have to admit, the idea of using a someday ring to promote our new song, "Someday," is pretty brilliant.

"Can't think of anything better." I flash a tight grin as Ezer hands Tinsley her guitar, and from the moment she starts singing, a genuine hush falls over the room.

There's no denying who the real talent is here.

Her voice is strong and captivating, and there's no doubt she has *it*—that indefinable thing that makes people want to watch her, listen to her, be near her.

As I watch Tinsley sing, it's easy to forget about the ring and all the weirdness that followed.

It's also easy to forget I'm not supposed to just sit here, I'm supposed to join in.

I pick up a little late, but since it's a new song, Tinsley and Ezer are the only ones who notice. And by the time we're well into the final refrain, all of the earlier tension is gone, leaving me feeling genuinely happy just to share this moment with her.

Which is why I'm caught completely off guard when she leans in to kiss me.

Like, *kiss* me kiss me.

Lips lingering.

Moving.

The kind of kiss that could never be considered a press-and-run.

Since I've never done this before, I just follow her lead until she pulls away, angles her face toward the camera, and giggles adorably.

And that's when I realize my very first kiss was just broadcast all over the world to millions of viewers.

Which makes me wonder if this was staged too.

Did Tinsley even want to kiss me—or was it just part of the script she was given?

I sit there stupidly, unsure what to do.

I mean, what's the correct response when your first kiss has been hijacked as a publicity stunt?

But it's not like it matters. Just a few seconds later the director calls it a wrap, Ezer grabs Tinsley's guitar, someone else unhooks my mike, and the crew begins dismantling the set as I make a mad dash upstairs to my room.

30

REALITY BITES

Once I'm in my room, I do something I should've done a long time ago: I watch the more recent episodes of my reality show. After everything that just happened, I need to know how I ended up diving straight off a metaphorical cliff without any warning.

I settle onto my bed with my laptop, and it doesn't take long before I'm gaping in horror at the way the camera captures my changed expression whenever Tinsley enters a scene.

Not to mention how they edit the smallest, most insignificant moments to make them seem way bigger than they actually were.

Clearly Ezer's had an agenda from the day he introduced

me to Tinsley, and he's been manipulating the footage ever since. He even added video clips of us goofing off in the recording studio when I was totally unaware of being filmed. Including shots of me trying to make her laugh and using any excuse to touch her arm, her shoulder, and one time— her knee. Making it seem like Tinsley and I have been a thing long before tonight.

Like we've been boyfriend and girlfriend all along.

Like the next logical step in our relationship would be for me to give her a someday ring.

And that's when I get the full extent of just how bad this mess is.

Ezer's been using me as a tool to make Tinsley famous.

I tell myself I shouldn't care.

I'm so well-known there's plenty to spare.

Still, I can't help feeling betrayed by the way he played me—how he used my feelings for her to manipulate me into going along with his game.

But mostly I'm mad at myself for allowing it, for not paying closer attention, for choosing to believe in this fake version of my life just as much as the fans who obsessively watch it.

And the worst part of all: after watching the footage, I can't help but realize that Tinsley isn't really the person I thought she was.

I guess I fooled myself into believing that if I could get someone as perfect as Tinsley to like me, then maybe it would make me perfect too. But now I know I had it all wrong. Tinsley's not even close to being perfect, and she only pretended to like me. A real friend would never use me like that. Tinsley's only in it for what she can get.

I reach for my cell, desperately needing to talk to someone, but the truth is, there's no one to call.

Despite all of my fortune and fame, turns out, I'm lonelier here than I ever was back in Greentree.

While the Greentree Dougall would understand, this Dougall is exactly what Ezer warned me about. He's only my friend for the celebrity perks. Always there to party and be seen with me, he's never around for the more normal, less flashy moments. Not to mention how he's always making fun of my music, my image, my decision to sing with Tinsley. And even though in retrospect he might've been right about the duet, I'm sick of him always urging me to collect the cash while I can and not giving a flying flip about anything else.

I may have a manager; a chauffeur/bodyguard; a chef, a personal stylist; a hair and makeup team; and a crew of people to mow my lawn, clean my pool, and keep my house organized and pristine, but I don't have anyone I can truly call a friend.

No one I can talk to about anything deeper than which party is worth going to and which girls make the hot list.

And as far as my family goes, well, I'm pretty sure I can't trust them. Heck, we couldn't even manage to have breakfast together. Not to mention how they clearly knew exactly what Ezer had planned and did nothing to protect me or, at the very least, warn me that I was about to be ambushed on live TV.

I mean, what kind of parents let their son get engaged, or promised, or *somedayed*, or whatever just happened to me, at almost thirteen?

What kind of mom claps her hands like it's the best news ever?

To think I'd actually felt guilty about not spending enough time with them, when the truth is, they never try to spend time with me. When my dad offers to take me golfing, or my mom and Holly say we should all do lunch—they're just repeating whatever it says in the script. Not a single one of them has bothered to follow up. No one has ever once pulled me aside to ask how I'm doing—how I'm really truly doing. No one has said anything original to me this whole, entire time.

They're just like everyone else here in Tinsel Hills—interested only in how I can benefit them.

Plum is probably the closest thing to a friend that I have in this place. And it's entirely possible she's been trying to nudge me toward the truth all along—in her own highly judgmental, sarcastic way, of course, which made it all too easy to tune her out.

I consider calling her—Dougall insisted on adding her number to my new phone in case his battery ran out and he was desperate to reach her—but after the look she gave me tonight, just after the ring was revealed, well, even though she was the only one willing to tell me the truth, I'm way too embarrassed to call and admit she was right about everything.

As it turns out, I really am the worst kind of sellout.

Willing to turn my back on everything I knew and loved just so I could continue deluding myself.

My real parents would never have let this happen.

My mom would have been outraged.

My dad would have ordered Ezer to leave.

Even Holly wouldn't have wanted me to make a fool of myself on TV.

Or maybe she would have. But at least she wouldn't have acted like the someday ring was great news.

The Greentree Holly would have shaken her head and said, "Nick—seriously, are you really that big of an idiot?"

Just thinking about my Greentree family has me missing them so much. I think I finally realize that it's better to be a real person than a flashy, hollow shell of one who lives a fake life. I roll off my mattress and barrel straight for the closet, where I plow through endless racks of designer clothes until I finally locate something from home. Then I slink back to bed with my hand-knit Christmas sweater clutched to my chest, relieved that I've managed to hang on to one small piece of the past.

There's a tentative knock on my door, followed by my mom asking for permission to enter.

If I close my eyes, I can hold the moment and pretend it's really her.

My Greentree mom.

But as soon as I open them again and see her perfect blond head poking in, the illusion is shattered.

"Nicky?" Her voice is so cloying it grates on my nerves. "You're trending on Twitter again!" She grins brightly, like she's the bearer of great news.

I roll my eyes and turn onto my side so I can no longer see her, but she doesn't get the hint and comes around to perch right beside me.

"Nicky." She runs a long, manicured nail over my sleeve and clasps my hand in hers. It's the only real motherly act she's displayed, and it makes me second-guess everything I was just thinking.

Maybe I'm just confused.

Maybe being constantly manipulated by Ezer has left me paranoid.

Maybe I was wrong about her.

Determined to give her a chance to prove she really does have my best interests at heart, I lift my chin to face her. But instead of saying something comforting, or even asking how I feel about everything that just happened, she crinkles her nose, takes a long withering look at the sweater still clutched in my arms, and says, "You're not planning to wear that . . . are you?"

I look at the sweater, try to see it through her eyes—same way I used to see it—as a complete and total embarrassment, something better left hidden. But I can no longer get there.

I shake my head, figuring if I give her the answer she

wants, then she'll leave me alone. "After all, it's better for me to trend on Twitter than my sweater, right?" I study her closely, watching as she fidgets and frowns. Ashamed by how I was so easily swayed by her actions, I failed to notice she was still empty inside.

She lets out a tight, high-pitched laugh and traces a nervous finger along the gold-and-diamond necklace I gave her. All the while she's patting my arm like you do when you're trying to appear comforting but all you really want to do is run far away and never look back.

Then she gets to her feet and heads for the door, acting like it's merely an afterthought and not the true purpose of her visit when she says, "Oh, and, Nicky—do you think you could front me some money? I'm a little short, and I won't have time to get to the bank now that the holiday rush has begun."

The question hangs heavy between us. Both of us know the show pays her plenty—way more than my real family would make if they owned a whole string of Dashaway Home and Hardware stores.

Still, I just point to my wallet and watch as she clears it of every last cent.

At first it seemed cool to be in charge. Living on my own with no curfew, no rules, no one to get in the way of my fun.

But the truth is, I don't need parents who depend on me.

I need parents I can depend on.

Once again Ezer was right: Dashing Nick Dashaway is

just another corporation with a slew of employees, including my family.

When the door closes behind her, I make sure to lock it.

I can't afford any more intrusions. It's time to plan my escape.

DECEMBER 24
12 Hours, 32 Minutes, and 2 Seconds
till Christmas

NINSLEY

By the next morning Tinsley and I are officially boyfriend and girlfriend.

I learned this via Twitter, where our relationship status is trending.

Depending on which Hollywood blog you read, we are either the most adorable couple on the planet—or the absolute lamest.

There's even a Twitter account for Tinsley's ring, with nearly a million followers.

It's projected to hit five million by the end of the day.

And don't even get me started on the Facebook fan pages and Tumblrs.

Not to mention that in the short span of time since the episode aired, more than a few of my most ardent fans have sent Tinsley death threats.

Ezer thinks it's great.

Tinsley too.

All I know for sure is that the fans have renamed us *Ninsley,* and I'm not sure how I feel about it, other than really, really weird.

I'm sitting by my pool when Ezer comes out to join me. "Nick!" he says. "Great news!"

I don't even bother to acknowledge him, but it's not like he notices.

"We did it, kid! It's official—we hit number one *and* number two!"

I shrug, unable to fake that I care.

"Hello? Did you hear me? The acoustic version hit number one—the studio version follows at number two! We own the charts, and the ratings went through the roof. Just like I predicted, 'Someday' had a million downloads before the credits stopped rolling. The media is in an absolute frenzy. Everyone's begging for interviews. You have no idea how much money you're about to make between now and New Year's Day. And the whole someday-ring scene"—he leans in so close I'm overcome by onion-bagel fumes—"genius. The girls are swooning. They all want to be Tinsley!"

"You mean the ones who aren't actually threatening to

kill her?" I look at Ezer, watching as he dismisses my words with a wave of his hand as though he doesn't find the threats the least bit disturbing.

"Crackpots, haters, and trolls are all part of the business. Tinsley knows not to take it seriously. She knows I'm looking out for her. She's also savvy enough to know it's the first sign of hitting the big time. Success breeds contempt, Nick. Always has, always will. There's no place for small minds in a big life. You gotta learn to ignore 'em. They're just sad little people with lives so miserable they project their hate elsewhere rather than taking a good, long look at themselves. The important thing is, at this very moment you and Tinsley are the names on everyone's lips!"

I lift a hand to shield my eyes from the sun so I can see him better. "Really?" I say. "That's the important thing?"

Ezer makes a face like he doesn't have time for my nonsense. "You'll thank me once you see the amount of money pouring into your bank account. Every time someone downloads your song, a cash register rings and an angel gets his wings!" He laughs at his joke for a lot longer than it warrants.

"Did Tinsley know about the ring?" I ask when he finally reels it in.

His face changes, switching from delighted to not-so-delighted in a handful of seconds. "What're you implying?"

"Just asking a question I'd really like answered."

Ezer's lips jerk to the side. It's one of his giveaways, and it's all I need to confirm my worst suspicions about him, about Tinsley, about me.

He rubs a hand over his chin and levels his gaze right on mine. No hiding, no nonsense. Finally. "What do you want me to say, Nick? I thought you understood how this works. If you're worried I'm going to rush Tinsley down the aisle at thirteen, think again. I wouldn't even consider it at eighteen, or twenty-one for that matter. So you can breathe easy. You don't have to marry her, Nick. You don't even have to see her after the show wraps tonight—other than for your contracted appearances, and of course when we begin filming *The Lazy Daze of Dashaway Summer Sizzle.* I think we can both agree, the timing works perfectly. Everyone loves a Christmas love story, not to mention a summer romance."

"And Tinsley's fine with all this? She's totally on board with pretending to like me and kiss me for the sake of the cameras?" For some reason the question sets me on edge. I guess because I'm not sure I'm ready for the answer.

But what I don't ask is: *Is that why Mac Turtledove disappeared so fast—because he couldn't help her become famous as quickly as I could?*

"Listen, Nick. The only reason I didn't fill you in sooner is because you have the soul of a true artist and it makes you emotional. It's what makes you a star—that ability to deeply immerse yourself in every experience. But it also keeps you from seeing things in a much broader, more logical way. Trust me, Nick, I've got it covered, and I always have your best interests at heart. So why don't you try to pull it together? We've got our Christmas finale to film in a matter of hours, and I need you on board. There's a huge surprise for you, Nick. And don't look at me like that—this is one I know you're gonna like. What do you say—you with me?" He leans closer, slaps a hand over my kneecap.

I meet his gaze and force myself to hold it until he's the first to look away. "Yeah," I say. "I'm all in." The lie comes easily.

"Glad to hear it." He grins and gets to his feet, blocking the sun in a way that casts a long, solid shadow to spill over me. "It's a busy day. There's a lot to prepare. But you get some rest, Nick. I need you in shape for tonight."

He's barely turned away when he starts barking into his phone, leaving me to wrestle with the truth I was trying to avoid.

The only reason Tinsley kissed me is because it was scripted.

32

8 Hours, 16 Minutes, and 11 Seconds
till Christmas

BYE-BYE, BIRDIE

A few hours later the only progress I've made is to chase the sun from my lounge chair to the edge of the pool, where I sit with my legs dangling knee-deep in the water, watching as a song sparrow uses the shallow end like it's his personal birdbath. This is how Tinsley finds me.

"Nick?" Her voice is tentative, her approach cautious, like she's afraid the slightest disturbance might set me off. "Lisa said I might find you out here."

I continue to watch the sparrow, my feet circling and churning the water.

"Nick?" She kneels down beside me. "How long have you been sitting like this? Your feet are seriously waterlogged."

She chases the words with a laugh that sounds more nervous than anything, and luckily she has the good sense to end it before it can really take hold. "You okay?" She places a hand on my leg.

I lift my gaze to meet hers, then focus on her hand resting on my jeans, that ridiculous sapphire someday ring glinting in the unnaturally bright sun until it practically blinds me.

"Oh, this." She lifts her hand between us. "It wasn't until I saw the look on your face that the reality set in. It was cruel to dupe you like that. But with the cameras rolling . . . well . . . I guess I just decided to follow the script and hope you'd play along, which you did, and I owe you big time for that."

"You don't owe me anything." I move my focus to her lips, remembering our kiss, but only for a moment before I return to watching the song sparrow fluff its feathers and take short drinks from the pool. "I mean, it worked, right? So what's to feel sorry about? It's my bad for not realizing sooner that I was just a pawn in your game."

"It's not a game, Nick." The words are sharp, and the look on her face is about as serious as I've ever seen. "This has been my dream for pretty much my whole entire life. I take it very seriously. I thought you did too."

"I did seriously dream of a different, better, much cooler life. I fully imagined myself living pretty much exactly like this." I gesture toward my sunshine-filled, palm tree-lined, fantasy yard. "Turns out, it isn't all it's cracked up to be."

She twists nervously at the ring on her finger, as though

she's afraid I might try to snatch it, taking her long-held dream of fame along with it. And that's when I realize just how much she has riding on this.

But I've got a lot at stake too.

"This life is borrowed," I say. "It's not really mine." I have no idea why I've decided to confess, other than it feels so good to speak the truth for a change after so much pretending. But to Tinsley's ears, my truth probably sounds cryptic and weird. It's completely out of context. And while I have no idea how to make her understand, that doesn't stop me from trying. "My life wasn't always like this." I attempt to explain the unexplainable. "I wasn't always an International Superstar. I wasn't always Dashing Nick Dashaway."

She mashes her lips together, drags her shoulders up toward her ears. "Well, everyone has to start somewhere. . . ."

"That's not what I mean." I'm suddenly overcome with the desperate need to be understood. "Up until five days ago, I lived in a place called Greentree, where I was a nobody. Invisible. An unpopular, overlooked Brainiac Nerd who couldn't get a single girl to look at me or like me, much less kiss me. Or, at least, not the kind of girl I wanted to kiss," I add, remembering Plum.

"Oh, I highly doubt that!" Tinsley plants an overly bright smile on her face—the kind that's normally reserved for when you accidentally start a conversation with a crazy person and are forced to mentally calculate the quickest escape route while trying not to alarm them. But I'm too far gone to stop now.

"You acted like I was invisible."

She shifts uncomfortably, looks over her shoulder toward the house. "Nick—this is getting weird." Her gaze is flat and discouraged. She's reached her limits, and she hasn't even heard the best part.

"Trust me, it's about to get even weirder. . . ."

I tell her about Josh Frost, the talent show, the magical cupcake, the bizarre Christmas trolley, the crazy driver with the tie-dyed red-and-green sweat suit and long white dreadlocks. I tell her that I'm pretty sure I've ended up in another dimension, another version of my life, but Tinsley's expression tells me she's simply stopped listening.

"Nick, I think we're all a little exhausted." She cuts me off, eager to be done with this. "But if we can just get through tonight's taping, we'll be free to finally relax and enjoy what's left of the holidays."

"And how exactly will we do that? Will Ezer script some nice romantic moments for us to share where we just so happen to have cinematographers on hand to capture every photogenic second, ensuring that *Ninsley* remains the number one couple the world is obsessing about? Will we head off on a snowy, romantic vacation together—just you, me, and Ezer?"

Her face pales. Her fingers continue to twist nervously, but it's not like it stops me.

"And, by the way, I can't help but wonder how Mac Turtledove feels about Ninsley becoming a thing. How exactly did you explain it to him? Or did Ezer do that for you?"

It's cruel, I know, but if I'm going to be honest, then I admit it's intended that way. I'm trying to push her into getting so upset she'll spill all the horrible truths she insists on keeping from me.

Or maybe I'm hoping she'll tell me I've got it all wrong. That despite how it looks, despite all the scripted nonsense, it really was her choice to kiss me. Maybe I'm hoping that she'll say all those things in a way that makes me believe them. So I can at least leave this place knowing I experienced one true thing out of so many fake, scripted ones.

In the end, she doesn't say anything. She just sighs in frustration, which says more than words ever could, confirming that my suspicions were true.

Turns out, she's not at all the person I wanted her to be.

She never really cared about me.

It was all just pretending.

Tinsley rises to her feet and leaves me to watch the song sparrow in silence.

He hops around a bit, takes a couple more sips, and trills so joyfully his whole body shivers. Then, after fluttering his wings, he lifts into flight—soaring beautifully, high and free—before crashing straight into the pool house window and snapping his neck, his lifeless body tumbling toward the cement.

33

5 Hours, 54 Minutes, and 13 Seconds
till Christmas

PLAYER GETS PLAYED

When I slide into the back of the limo, I make a mental inventory of all of my interactions with Sparks, hoping I haven't been too big of a pain, not counting the times in the beginning when I may have gone a little overboard with bossing him around. He's an integral part of my plan, which means that now, more than ever, I need him as an ally.

"You remember that place—that trolley stop—where you picked me up five days ago?" I push my face close to the divider, wanting to get a better look so I can gauge his reaction.

He shifts as though he's looking at me through the rearview mirror, but the reflective lenses he wears makes it impossible to confirm what he's thinking.

"You know, that day you were waiting for me because the trolley was late?" I add, really hoping he remembers, because I have no idea how to find it on my own.

Still nothing.

"I really need you to take me there. The sooner the better. And if Ezer calls, tell him you haven't seen me," I say, hoping he can glean from my tone, if not my actual words, just how urgent this is. I need to leave now, before Ezer has a chance to notice I'm gone, and hopefully well before my return ticket expires, which is just a few hours from now. I cast a nervous glance toward the street. It's just a matter of time before Ezer and the rest of the film crew arrive, thereby killing any chance I'll have of escaping this place.

Sparks rubs his lips together but otherwise makes no move to start the car and pull out of the drive.

"You sure about this, Nick?" he finally says. And it's probably the first thing he's ever said to me other than *You got it!*

Or *Watch your head!*

Or *I got you covered!*

Or *Ezer called—he wants you on set, immediately!*

Not to mention he called me Nick.

Not Mr. Dashaway, which I never fully got used to, but Nick.

Does that mean he's on my side?

Does that mean he knows the truth about how I found myself here in Tinsel Hills?

"Yeah," I tell him. "Never been more sure in my life."

And when he starts the engine and eases the limo onto

the street, I collapse against my seat, feeling like I can finally breathe.

I'm going home!

To Greentree!

And I can't get there quickly enough.

The streets are clogged with traffic, which would normally only add to my anxiety, but as long as we make it by one minute past midnight, when the ticket expires, I figure I'm good. The plan is to get there and find a place to lie low until the trolley arrives and hauls me right out of this life.

I pull my hoodie up over my head, prepping for the moment when the most famous teen in the world (me) attempts to go incognito. Then I sink down low in my seat and reach for what will probably turn out to be my last can of Mojo while I cradle my backpack on my knees as though it might try to flee.

Too bad I couldn't pack a bigger bag and take some of the awesomeness with me. But unfortunately the makeup, hair, and wardrobe people decided to arrive early, leaving me no choice but to sneak out when no one was looking.

The real Dougall would love the Xbox I got the other Dougall for Christmas. I found it in my room today with a sticky note attached, reading THANKS, BUT I ALREADY HAVE ONE.

And my dad could really use a fat wad of Ben Franklins to deal with his back taxes and year-end financials.

But Holly would've hated the Vespa. Turns out, it's pink.

And my mom would've felt really uncomfortable wearing

something as fancy and expensive as the diamond necklace I gave Eileen.

Not to mention how impossible it would be to explain all those things.

Still, it's kind of funny to have owned all the cool stuff money can buy, only to return home with the same stuff I arrived with and feel perfectly okay about it.

Besides, the return ticket is my most valuable possession anyway.

I trace the edge of the pocket where I stashed the ticket, reassured by the feel of it crinkling inside, as Sparks comes to a stop, slips from his seat, and walks around to my side. But before he can even reach for the handle, I'm opening the door, leaping toward freedom, only to gape in horror when I see he betrayed me.

"What the heck?" My first instinct is to pummel him, but he's ten times my size. "Do you have any idea what you've done?" I'm transfixed by the sight of Ezer's mansion looming large before me. "You work for *me*—not Ezer, me! And I'm ordering you to take me to the trolley stop immediately!"

But no matter what I say or how loudly I say it, Sparks is impenetrable. He just continues to watch me from behind his mirrored lenses. "You sure you got everything?"

"What? Of course! Now let's go, before someone sees me!"

I start to climb back inside the limo, but Sparks stays put. "Maybe you should double-check, Nick."

The way he says it makes my heart squeeze and my skin go all weird and tingly. Then he nods his head toward my bag just the tiniest bit. I'm overcome with this awful gnawing feeling—like my stomach grew teeth and they're cannibalizing me from the inside out.

I unzip the pocket, shove my fingers inside, and come away with a palmful of air, a stray ball of lint, and an old movie ticket stub I mistook for my ticket.

How can this even be possible?

It was in there last night before I went to bed, just after I came up with my plan. I checked to make sure!

I force the pocket inside out, and still all I unearth is another ball of lint and a really old gum wrapper with more lint stuck to it. So I reach for my backpack. Even though I've never once moved the ticket, that doesn't stop me from dropping to my knees and dumping the entire contents of my bag onto the ground, scrambling through every single item, if only to confirm that the return ticket is gone.

I gaze up at Sparks. *Desperation* doesn't even begin to describe the emotions raging inside me.

The side of his mouth twitches like he's just about to speak when Ezer opens the front door and calls for me to come inside immediately.

"Where is it?" I whisper, convinced Sparks has something to do with this. How else would he know the ticket was missing? "Please—if you know who took it, you've got to tell me. And if you took it, you need to return it!"

Sparks kneels down and helps me stuff my things back inside, as though they got there through some kind of unfortunate mishap.

Ezer calls from the doorway again and tells us to hurry. But Sparks just waves him away and leans toward me. "I didn't take it, Nick. But if you think about it, I'm sure you'll discover who did."

"Wait—what? What does that even mean?" My voice is frantic and shrieky, betraying the full extent of my panic.

"*Think,* Nick."

So I do. I conduct a full mental inventory of everyone who had access to my house.

The list is long.

Too long to really consider.

So I make another mental list, this one consisting of the people who would be determined to keep me here, who benefit merely by knowing me, who not only had access to my room but might even know what to look for.

Which narrows it down to . . . everyone. But since Tinsley got an earful out by my pool, maybe she's the top suspect?

Ezer shouts again, becoming really impatient, as Sparks grabs hold of my arm, pulls me to my feet, and pushes me toward the house, where Ezer and Tinsley are waiting.

DASHAWAY HOME

34

4 Hours, 14 Minutes,
and 28 Seconds
till Christmas

SURPRISED FACE

I reach the front door, and Ezer says, "Nick—what gives? I called you countless times, Sparks too, but neither of you had the decency to answer. You'd think you could at least save this kind of behavior for your break, which starts tomorrow, by the way. Is that too much to ask?"

No matter how worked up he gets, his voice is just noise in my head. I'm too busy gaping at the HAPPY BIRTHDAY, NICK! banner hanging overhead. Not to mention the Christmas decorations, and the cast, crew, and cameras all standing by, ready to shoot.

Ezer set me up!

And Sparks helped him.

But he also helped me by pointing out the missing ticket and bringing me here for a chance to retrieve it.

All I know for sure is that the *Twelve Days of Dashaway Christmas Countdown* finale is being shot here.

Which means either that Ezer wasn't one bit fooled by our conversation by the pool or that Tinsley told him everything I was dumb enough to tell her, or both.

In the end it doesn't matter how he knew. He's been pulling the strings all along. Probably has my ticket hidden in his pocket, and there's nothing I can do about it. It's not like I can tackle him to the ground and demand that he return it. I bet he has a whole security team waiting for me to try.

"So!" He slaps a hand to my back, using more force than necessary. "Bet you thought we forgot your birthday in all the excitement." His grin is so tight and wide it reminds me of a cartoon shark zeroing in on its prey. "That's why we changed the location—we wanted to surprise you. We're set for one heck of a party to celebrate *you*, Nick! But first—what's this you're wearing?"

He pinches my sleeve between his index finger and thumb as I gaze down at the hoodie I grabbed in a hurry. Same hoodie I was wearing under the Christmas sweater when I first arrived here. The faded blue one with *Greentree M.S.* written in yellow script along the right side.

He squints. Probably trying to figure out the best way to tell me to change, that the color washes me out or doesn't play well on TV—the usual excuses when he doesn't like what I'm wearing.

"I have no idea where you found it," he says, "but it works! It's old school. Random. Doesn't look overly stylized, like you're trying too hard. You're just teenage Nick Dasha-way walking into your surprise party. A hoodie like that says you don't take yourself too seriously. You don't feel the need to overdo it every time you leave your house. It's like giving the viewer an insider's look at the real you. It's genius, I tell you! Nothing phonier than some celebrity visiting a friend wearing a tuxedo and bow tie."

I nod. Shrug. I had no idea a single hoodie could convey all of that.

He continues to study me with a deepening gaze. "You know, my first reaction was to tell you to change. But some-times it's good to take a step back and look at things from a whole new perspective. Oftentimes you'll find that the things that once bothered you aren't nearly as bad as you think. In fact, once we get past our initial resistance, we're able to see that our situation may actually be a whole lot better than we originally thought. So much so that we would never consider going back to doing things the old way. Know what I mean?"

All I know for sure is that at some point this conversa-tion switched from being about the hoodie to being about me. I nod, willing to agree to just about anything until I can get my hands on that ticket and get the heck out of here.

"Why don't you go on over to hair and makeup so we can get ready to roll. Then head back outside and ring the bell. And this time, when we jump out and shout, 'Surprise!' I want you to look as shocked as you did when you first arrived."

★

Back when I was eleven and three quarters and about to start my first year of middle school, my dad warned me about the absolute foolishness of assuming.

"Never assume you know what another person is thinking or feeling," he said. "Bullies bully not because they feel strong but because they feel powerless inside. And the people you view as popular don't have perfect, problem-free lives. Nobody does."

He went on to demonstrate how the very word itself is a warning. It's all right there in the spelling, impossible to ignore: *ass-u-me*. And yet people still choose not to see it and assume all kinds of things, about all kinds of people, on a regular basis.

It's not like I didn't listen. But at the time, all I really got from that talk was that my dad feared I'd be marked as unpopular bully bait from day one and felt the need to prepare me.

It's only now that I truly get the lesson.

Too bad it's too late to change the fact that I assumed I could outwit Ezer and this dream life, only to have them outwit me.

Though it's not the only assumption I've made. I've assumed all kinds of things about everyone here, and now it's time to challenge at least one of them.

It's a really big risk that could very well backfire, but with Ezer tracking my every move, I have no choice but to go on with the show. Which means if I've any hope of pulling this off, I'll have to narrow my list of suspects and pin all my hopes on the one person I'm not even sure I can trust but is the only one who might be willing to help me.

★

With my hair purposely messy and my face powdered down, I stand outside Ezer's front door waiting for the director to shout, "Action!" That's my cue to enter wearing a surprised face while Eileen clasps me tightly to her chest and wipes nonexistent tears from her cheeks as she reminisces about the miraculous day she brought her little Christmas miracle (that would be me) into the world and how she knew right away I was destined to be a star.

Joe stands alongside us, beaming for the camera while droning on about how proud I've made him. Until the camera pans to focus on the fake Sir Dasher Dashaway dancing circles at my feet, and Joe drops the proud expression for one of extreme boredom, like he'd much rather be hitting balls on the course than praising me on TV.

Holly takes the Santa hat from her own head and plops it on mine, all the while recounting some staged story about my absolute adorableness as a baby, which comes off as so freaking lame I'm embarrassed for all of us. I mean, what self-respecting sister would ever say such a thing?

Do people actually believe this stuff?

Was I this gullible when I watched the Josh Frost show?

And am I the only one bothered by the complete lack of reality in my reality show?

Where were the cameras when my mom was dissing my sweater and raiding my wallet?

And how come no one ever thinks to film one of Ezer's incessant lectures or meltdowns?

Heck, even Sir Dasher Dashaway got a stunt double when he overindulged and ended up hurling his cookies all over the floor.

If it doesn't appear perfect—or at least charmingly imperfect—it won't make the cut.

And I guess that's what bugs me the most. All this time I longed for a perfect life surrounded by perfect people, only to discover that a real life, a good life, is anything but.

Still, I do my best to play along. For one thing, I can't afford to alarm Ezer any more than I already have. I need to convince him he can trust me—that I'm fully committed—that I've come to my senses and wouldn't even consider messing up a good thing. Problem is, I'm not that good an actor. But with my future happiness on the line, I'll do whatever it takes.

It's not until the fake Dougall goes for a fist bump, mumbling, "Happy birthday, bro! So glad you made it," that I get all choked up. Not because I believe he gives a flying flip about my birthday but because it makes me miss the old Dougall, who always means what he says. Though by the time I reach the end of the line where Tinsley waits, looking impossibly pretty, I've got my emotions in check.

"Happy birthday, Nick." She leans in to kiss me.

But as irresistible as she seems with her eyes closed and her lips willing and ready, I turn my head so her lips land on my cheek, making it more like a kiss from your nana than a kiss from the girl you've wasted the last year and a half dreaming about. When she pulls away, trying to hide her own surprised face, I whisper, "Thanks, Tins." My eyes bore into hers as if to silently say, *I know what you did.*

"Cut!" the director yells, insisting we shoot it again. "You're in love! So deeply in love you gave her a someday ring! Come on, Ninsley—show the fans what first love looks like!" He tries to ignite a flame that'll never spark again.

Inwardly I roll my eyes. Still, you have to pick your battles in life, and this one isn't at all worth the fight. We're on a tight schedule. Everyone wants to go home and spend the holiday with their family, me included.

This time I let Tinsley kiss me. Starting a slow countdown from three to one the second her lips touch mine, then moving straight into the scene where we're pretending to be relaxed and happy, until my parents and Holly disappear into the kitchen, only to return with the most humongous birthday cake I've ever seen. And that's when I realize, at this exact moment, my every wish has come true. Tinsley is my girlfriend—I'm the most famous teen in the world—and my birthday is no longer overshadowed by the holiday.

Only now that I have all that, I feel ashamed for having wanted it.

The candles sizzle like sparklers as Tinsley presses near.

"Make a wish, Nick," she says. "Sometimes wishes come true!"

My gaze locks on hers, caught by her words. This is pretty much how I found myself here.

Maybe it was only a cupcake instead of an actual cake.

And instead of thirteen stunt candles, there was only one red-and-green one.

But the ritual is the same.

There's power in a wish, Plum said. *Don't waste it on the mundane.*

Tinsley grasps my hand, her grip a little too forced, the squared edges of her perfectly manicured nails digging into my palm. "You're going to burn down the house if you don't blow those out! Hurry! Make a wish, Nick—and make it a good one!"

"Make a wish!" Dougall calls.

"Make a wish, Nicky!" my fake mom says.

"What's the matter, Nick? Your life so great you've got nothing left to wish for?" Ezer taunts from the sidelines.

I stare at the candles.

What if this is my way out—like a glamorous bookend to my earlier experience?

What if this is the one thing that can turn it all around?

What if that ticket doesn't even matter?

What if it really is this easy?

I take one last look at Ezer, close my eyes, and make my wish, emptying my lungs of every last ounce of air I have in me.

35

3 Hours, 3 Minutes,
and 33 Seconds
till Christmas

REINDEER GAMES

Ever hear the saying lightning never strikes twice?

Turns out it's true.

The second I blow out the candles and open my eyes, it's clear that not a single thing has changed.

The cameras are still rolling. Tinsley is still standing beside me, her voice a little nervous and hitched. "Try not to look so disappointed, Nick! What did you wish for—to be teleported to a beach in Hawaii?"

I shoot a quick glance at Ezer before returning to Tinsley. Smiling brightly for the camera, I slide my arm around her, and in my most charming Nick Dashaway voice, say, "Why would I want to be anywhere but right here beside *you?*"

Her eyes meet mine, and though her smile is tight like she suspects something's up, she's professional enough to make little squealing sounds as she springs onto her toes and kisses my cheek.

I do my best to go along. As the only one in the room who didn't get the handout, I have no idea what's to come. Still, if there's one thing I know about TV, it's that the biggest reveals are always saved for the season finale, where they love to throw in a cliffhanger. And judging by the way Ezer's acting, I've no doubt he's got something planned.

But I have something planned too.

I continue to go through the motions. Even when we film the scene where Dougall and I are messing around, singing "Jingle Bells" to the tune of "Twelve Days," and I'm reminded of a similar scene back in Greentree when the real Dougall walked in on me as I was rehearsing in my bedroom, and how instead of making fun of me he just looked at me and said, "I still think you're crazy for wanting to get up in front of the entire school and sing, but I gotta admit, you sound almost good"—even though I know this Dougall would never support me like that, that he's my friend only because of the girls and the gifts and the way our friendship benefits him—I still keep my cool.

I keep playing along for the cameras like everything's normal until Plum enters the room and I no longer have to.

I glare at Ezer, ready to call him out for stealing the ticket and making Tinsley hide it, when I realize that Plum didn't arrive on her own. One of Ezer's bodyguards has dragged her in by the arm.

"Found her up in Tinsley's room, going through her stuff," he says.

And just like that, my plan falls apart.

"Is this true?" Ezer approaches Plum, but to her credit she doesn't say a word. Doesn't even implicate me by looking my way.

"Caught her with her hand right inside Tinsley's purse. How do you want to handle it?" The security guy tightens his grip on Plum's arm like he's hoping Ezer will command him to haul her off to prison or worse.

Ezer rubs a hand over his chin and studies Plum. "Why would you do that?" He acts as though the question is for her until he turns and his gaze levels on me.

He knows.

He knows I put her up to it.

Since he thwarted my original plan to make a run for the trolley stop, I was forced to act so quickly I didn't have time to brainstorm a backup plan in case this one failed.

He knows this is the only card in my deck. Now he's daring me to admit it.

"She did it because I asked her to," I say. "I sent her a text asking her to go through Tinsley's purse and get something Tinsley took from me."

Tinsley gasps. Like, audibly gasps. And from the sound of it, this time she's not acting.

"And why would you do that?" Ezer's expression shifts so quickly it's hard to keep track, but one thing's for sure: he's offering a challenge I have no choice but to meet.

"Because Plum's the only one I can trust. She's the only one who doesn't want something from me. Heck, she doesn't even like me."

I sneak a look at Plum. I can't help it. And considering how much trouble she's facing, it's kind of nice to see she's still able to grin.

"Nick—what's going on with you?" Tinsley's pretty face turns pink with betrayal and outrage. "First you accuse me of stealing from you, then you claim you can't trust me. Is that what you think? That I'm with you only for what I can get?" She looks as though she's asking me to deny it, which is kind of funny, considering our earlier conversation where she made it perfectly clear that those accusations are true.

The whole room goes silent as everyone waits for my response.

And that's when I realize that the cameras never stopped rolling. Everything that's happening here is being recorded.

This is Ezer's ultimate test.

His final manipulation.

He's pushing me to choose a life lived as Dashing Nick Dashaway, International Superstar—or to outright reject it and risk never returning to Greentree.

If I make the choice he wants, he'll edit out the bad parts and I'll continue living the dream.

If not, he'll make sure the whole mess goes viral so I'll be forced to live out my life in disgrace, stuck in this place with a family that doesn't like me and even fewer friends than I had back in Greentree.

He's making me bet on my future.

The outcome is mine to decide.

I glance between Ezer, Plum, and Tinsley. My heart hammering hard in my chest, I take a step closer and say, "Where are you hiding it, Tins?"

"I don't know what you're talking about." She insists on denying what we both know is true.

"I think you do." I look right at her, unable to see her the same way I used to. She's a better singer than me, and definitely a better actor, since all along she's been playing me.

"Nick!" She lets out a high-pitched squealy sound—a cross between a scream and a laugh. "What's in that mug of hot chocolate you're drinking?" She points a shaky finger toward the red-and-green cup bearing my name. "You're acting all crazy!"

It's a desperate attempt to insert a little humor, make it seem like a brief moment of insanity before we all return to our regularly scheduled programming. Too bad it won't work. For me there's no turning back.

"The ticket, Tins. I confided in you today by the pool when I told you about the cupcake magic and the crazy Christmas trolley and how I found myself here."

"Nick ..." She presses a hand to her throat and slowly backs away, the camera continuing to track our progress as I match her every step. "Nick, *please*!" Her fingers twist nervously at the someday ring, like she doesn't know whether to protect it or to hurl it at me.

"The ticket expires one minute past midnight, time's running out, and I want to spend Christmas in my real home, with my real family. Not this"—oblivious to the camera recording every word, I point at Joe, Eileen, and Holly—"not this embarrassing, plasticized version of a family."

"Hey, now—that was uncalled for!" Joe shouts in outrage as Holly glares and Eileen clutches her diamond necklace as though I might snatch it right off her neck.

But it's not enough to stop me. Not even close.

"And this"—I pause, unsure how to refer to Dougall—"this fake, wannabe-celebrity friend."

He holds his hands up before him, glancing between the camera and me, saying, "Whoa, bro—that is seriously harsh!"

Despite the cruel things I just said about my family and friends, the biggest upset comes when I refer to Sir Dasher Dashaway as a completely ridiculous embarrassment of a dog. Even the film crew is outraged. But it's all just background noise. I no longer care about my image or how this will play on TV. I'm determined to get the heck out of here so I can go back to my life as a Brainiac Nerd, supported by people I've only just now learned to appreciate, and Tinsley is the single person who can either help or hurt me.

"It's not too late to fix this," I tell her.

But one look at her face tells me she has completely shut down.

And when Mac Turtledove appears on the sidelines, taking his place beside Ezer, I'm not one bit surprised to see how, just like in Greentree, he ends up with the girl and the life I dreamed of having.

As far as I'm concerned, it's his for the taking.

Tinsley heaves a resigned sigh, pulls her hand from her pocket, and thrusts it toward me.

But instead of the ticket I was expecting, she removes the sapphire ring from her finger and drops it onto my palm, allowing the camera to zoom in for a close-up before she folds my fingers around it.

"Sorry, Nick." Her eyes mist with tears—she's gotten really good at crying on cue. "I guess we were wrong about each other. This no longer feels right. Besides, I'm too young to be promising myself to anyone. But *someday* ... when we're both older and more mature, who knows?"

Someday.

Nice way to plug our #1 and #2 hits.

She turns away, blond hair sailing behind her like a curtain being drawn.

She no longer needs me—Mac Turtledove's waiting.

It's enough to satisfy Ezer too.

Because just after that, the director shouts, "Cut—that's a wrap!"

Ezer shakes his head, then shows me the door.

36

57 Minutes and 42 Seconds
till Christmas

REALITY REFUGEE

For someone who has spent the last five days being chased by screaming fans, it feels kinda strange to transition into a social pariah in just a matter of seconds. Though I guess I better get used to it. If I don't get my hands on that ticket, this is how I'll live out my days, without a single person willing to speak to me.

Tinsley hates me for humiliating her on TV.

My family hates me for calling them embarrassing and plastic, but most of all for the lifestyle they'll lose because of my choices.

And when I tried to apologize to Plum, her mom stood in my way and told me she quit.

"You surprise me, kid." Ezer walks behind me, practically clipping my heels. "I thought you were smarter than that."

I toss my mike and head for the door, determined to find my way to the trolley stop and try pleading my case with the driver. It's the only hope I have left. "I guess it's like you once said," I tell him. "Nothing wrong with knowing your limits. I guess I discovered mine."

"You know you just committed celebrity suicide, right? By tomorrow morning every girl in America—heck, the whole world—will have turned against you. You cleared the decks for Mac to step in and take your place. And I gotta admit, the kid's got charisma. Won't be long before they forget about Ninsley and start screaming for Macsley."

His words stop me cold.

I realize the one thing I've missed all along, even though it was sitting right smack in front of me.

Ezer is the only one here who's exactly the same as he was back in Greentree.

"You're in on it, aren't you?" I have no way to explain it or prove it, but I know that I'm right. "You've known the whole time."

"What I know, kid, is you've killed your career and I no longer represent you. After the stunt you just pulled, won't be long before all your other deals drop you as well. You'll be lucky if you can scrape together enough dough to rent a small apartment somewhere. And you better make sure they take pets, since you put your family's financial well-being at risk, which means they'll be living with you. You'll be broke in no time—and with a face as recognizable as yours, good luck blending into the world. The one thing that always bothered you—the lack of privacy—will never be yours. People know who you are. They watched your meltdown unfold on TV. From this moment on there's nowhere to hide."

It's all true.

Every single word.

Which is why it's imperative for me to make one final plea.

"None of this has to happen," I say. "Just give me that ticket and you can pretend we never met."

He stands before me, as impenetrable as a brick wall, his henchmen watching from a few feet away, in case I'm dumb enough to try to jump him or something.

"Why won't you help me?" I ask, refusing to give up so easily.

"I did help you." He slaps me hard on the back. "I gave you a life most people can only dream of, and this is how you repay me. Good luck, Nick. You're gonna need it." He shuts the double doors firmly between us, and from the corner of my eye I see Dougall making his way down the drive.

"Hey!" I rush to catch up. "Hey—Dougall!" I call, wanting to apologize for what I said on TV. Just because it's true doesn't make it okay to share with the world. "Dougall?"

I quicken my pace, only to watch as he quickens his as well. Reaching the end of the drive well before me, he slips through the electronic gate just as it's closing and laughs when it slams shut in my face.

And that's when it hits me.

I had it all wrong.

Ezer and Tinsley didn't steal the ticket.

They just used my story and pending meltdown to reframe the show, to make room for Mac.

And though my family had plenty of motive, they looked way too clueless to be involved either.

But Dougall—

Dougall was alone in my room when he returned the Xbox earlier today. He could have overheard me by the pool spilling my guts to Tinsley.

Dougall's entire life, his whole identity, revolves around being my friend.

If I return to Greentree, where does that leave him?

Also, what was that he said just after wishing me a happy birthday? Something about how he was glad to see that I'd made it?

As if there was any doubt that I would? As if I've ever failed to show up?

He expected me to run.

All the while knowing I wouldn't get very far.

"Why'd you do it?" I grab hold of the thick iron bars, shaking them as hard as I can, but the gate refuses to budge.

He drops his skateboard to the ground and places his foot on the deck. "Don't bother." He motions toward my futile attempt. "You're not going anywhere, Nick." He reaches into his pocket and wags the trolley ticket in my face. His eyes narrowed, his grin crooked and wide, he milks the moment for all he can. "Figured you'd blame Tinsley and Ezer once you caught on to their reality game. Which took you a ridiculously long time, by the way. All those failed attempts to kiss her because Ezer interfered—you think that was a coincidence?" He shakes his head. "Anyone could see she was using you, but you were so hung up on your fantasy version of Tinsley you chose to ditch me, your best bro, just so you could spend more time with a girl who never even liked you. I was willing to let it go for a while, since I figured you'd wise up soon enough, but then I overheard you talking to Tinsley about how you got here and how much you want to return. . . ."

He thrusts the ticket toward me until it's almost within reach, but just as I make a move for it, he yanks it back again.

"You seriously thought I'd let you rob me of this life?" He looks at me like I'm the biggest moron he's ever seen. "We had everything—an all-access, red-carpet, VIP pass to the whole entire world! But apparently that wasn't good enough for you, since you can't wait to leave it all behind. Tell me, Nick, out of all the time you've spent feeling sorry for yourself, did you ever stop to think about me? Did you ever once consider what might happen to me when you leave?"

I can't meet his glare, so I stare down at my shoes. There's no denying he's right. I didn't think about him. He never once factored into my decision.

"And now, thanks to you, I'm about to become a complete and total nobody." He shakes his head and scowls. "No, scratch that, I'll be worse than a nobody—I'll be a joke—a has-been—the celebrity suck-up who got dumped by his best bro on TV. Nice work, Dashaway."

"You can always try to get in good with Mac Turtledove. . . ." The second it's out I regret it. I meant to present it as a viable option, but it sounded more like an insult. "Dougall, listen—" I rush to cover, but he won't let me finish.

"All you had to do was stick with Ezer's plan for a couple more years, three at the most. Just keep riding the fame wave until the tide turned and someone new took your place. Is that too much to ask?"

I study him for a long moment. Deciding to go with the truth. "As it turns out, yes."

He flips his skateboard up with his foot, then angrily slams it back down. "Wrong answer, Nick. Anyway, enjoy living the rest of your life as a nobody. I know I won't, but if I'm going down, I'm taking you with me." He shoots me a sickly grin, tucks the ticket into his pocket, and speeds down the street, disappearing from view.

37

38 Minutes and 18 Seconds
till Christmas

SK8TR BOY

I shake the gate again, but it hardly even moves. And since there's no one inside Ezer's house who would be willing to help, I hoist myself onto one of the thick iron scrolls and use it as a foothold to heave myself up.

"Well, one thing's for sure, we'll definitely break all existing records as the most talked-about season finale."

Tinsley.

"Nothing like a little controversy to raise the ratings and get people talking. And just so you know, it's already gone viral. Ezer has had the crew feeding clips to YouTube since the whole thing fell apart—all done anonymously, of course. But I know you no longer care about that."

I focus on the gate and continue to climb.

"The someday ring was ridiculous, completely over-the-top."

I heave myself up, but the gate is so tall, there's still a long way to go.

"And, just so you know, I really did try to talk Ezer out of going through with it. I mean, we're not even thirteen!"

"Tins—" I turn to find her fidgeting with something inside her pocket, which only confuses me more. What could she possibly be hiding? What kind of game is she playing? I already know Dougall stole the ticket.

"Then again, even though it was dumb, it definitely worked. Whatever you may think of him, he is a genius when it comes to making headlines."

I heave a frustrated sigh, making no attempt to hide my annoyance. Tinsley is seriously starting to get on my nerves.

"Still, I want you to know that, while the ring may have been fake, my feelings for you weren't—or at least, not entirely. Remember that day on the beach? Remember what I said to you?"

I center my foot and reach for a handhold, pausing long enough to remember the day she looked at me and said, *Promise me that no matter what happens, you'll remember this moment. . . .*

"I really did mean it. I really did want to kiss you."

I close my eyes briefly. Five days ago I dreamed of hearing Tinsley Barnes say those words.

Today they're just another delay I cannot afford.

"But I understand if you're into Plum. I'm sure she's perfectly nice once you get to know her."

I shake my head. That's where she's got it all wrong. "There's nothing perfect about Plum." I pull myself up another two feet. "But that's what makes her so cool. She never tries to pretend to be something she's not."

Tinsley grows quiet, taking that in. "Sounds like you really like her," she says, and, if I'm not mistaken, she sounds a bit jealous.

"I don't even know her," I reply, realizing it's true.

"Anyway . . ." Tinsley pauses so long that for a moment I think she might've gone. But she remains right in place, hand shoved into her pocket, as she sways from side to side. "I just wanted you to know that," she says. "You know, before you go away for good."

I squint, not quite understanding.

"I swear I had nothing to do with it. I'm not even sure I believe this Greentree place really exists."

She lifts her face toward me, and between the soft golden glow of the yard lights below and the shining full moon above, she's probably the prettiest I've ever seen her, and that's saying a lot. Only it no longer affects me the way it once did.

"Come down from there, Nick."

I pause, unsure what to do.

"There's no way you can get past those spikes at the top without causing some serious damage to yourself. Those aren't decoration, you know."

I look up and see that she's right. In my rush to flee, I never once considered how I'd get past those razor-sharp points.

I drop to the ground. Aided by gravity and the weight of defeat, I land before Tinsley.

"Before I open the gate, just tell me one thing—" She slips her hand from her pocket, revealing the remote control she holds in her palm. "What's she like? You know, the other me—the one you told me about by the pool. Is she nice?" Her voice lifts with hope, like we're just two normal people having a conversation about an alternate world.

"I don't know," I admit. "I've never even talked to her. She has no idea I exist."

"Then she must be an idiot." Tinsley grins.

"Nah, she's just a girl." I shrug, realizing the same goes for this version of Tinsley. I convinced myself she was perfect, then pretty much the opposite of perfect, only to realize she's like most people—somewhere in the middle.

Her face grows thoughtful, then more resolved, as she pushes the button that opens the gate. And just as I'm about to slip past, she calls me right back. "Will this help?" She pulls a skateboard from the bushes and offers it to me. "I keep it hidden so I can sneak away when Ezer gets on my nerves, but I can always get a new one."

"Thanks." I flip it into my hand and sprint for the street like my life depends on it.

It does.

38

24 Minutes and 52 Seconds
till Christmas

VULTURE, MEET PREY

The worst thing about being an International Superstar on the run is that I'm easily recognized.

The second worst thing is that I'm so used to being chauffeured around town I have no idea how to navigate the city on my own.

And to make matters worse, I pretty much suck at skateboarding.

Then again, I'm really not that great of a singer either, and in this dimension I'm considered one of the best. So maybe it'll be the same with skating.

Turns out it's not.

Still, that doesn't keep me from barreling down the

Tinsel Hills sidewalks in search of Dougall and the stolen ticket. Though considering how he rides a skateboard more often than me (from what I've seen, it's pretty much his go-to mode of transportation when Sparks isn't chauffeuring us around), he definitely has the competitive edge. I mean, I barely ever ride the skateboard I own back in Greentree.

Despite the late hour, the streets are surprisingly busy, and I've barely gone a few blocks when I spot a crowd of paparazzi swarming the corner just a few feet ahead, as drawn to my failure as they were to my success. My blood is in the water, and every shark in the vicinity is swimming right for me.

I'm just about to change course when I see Dougall trapped in the center of them. The paparazzi jostle around him like vultures hunting their prey.

This is perfect.

They've got him right where I want him.

It wouldn't take much to jump him and steal the ticket right out from under him. The paparazzi wouldn't even try to stop me. They'd be too busy filming.

I curl my hands into fists, ready to pounce at the first opportunity.

"Tell me, Dougall," one of them shouts. "Is it true you were only pretending to be Nick's friend so you could enjoy all the perks?"

What?

That's not at all what I said. Though, if I'm going to be honest, I have to admit it was definitely what I implied. It's how I've felt this whole time.

"Dougall, hey—over here!" Another one shoves his camera into Dougall's face. "Are you really just another wannabe celebrity?"

Before Dougall can respond, another one edges in. "What will you do, now that your former best friend has turned his back on everyone, you included?"

I freeze, unsure what to do. I had every intention of knocking Dougall down to get my hands on that ticket, but now, seeing the way the photogs harass him, I can't help but feel like this is my fault. If I hadn't done what I did, said what I said—if I hadn't called him out as an insincere fake on TV, he wouldn't find himself at the center of a paparazzi feeding frenzy.

All I wanted was to return home to Greentree, and in my desperation I went completely overboard with the insults.

Dougall holds his skateboard before him, wielding it like a shield, as his eyes dart frantically in search of escape.

He looks trapped.

Scared.

A little confused.

He looks like a kid who wanted a crack at the spotlight with no idea of the cost.

A kid just like me.

I check the time on my cell. With only thirteen minutes to spare, it's not looking good. And yet there's no way I can go, knowing I've left him to deal with this mess on his own.

I speed toward them, fighting like heck to stay upright, and it doesn't take long before Dougall sees me and shouts,

"Hey—Nick's the one you really want, and he's right behind you!"

In less than a second, they surround me in a hail of flashbulbs and taunts, and now that the focus is off him, Dougall hangs around to see how it plays out.

"Nick! Nick—over here!"

"Why did you do that, Nick? Why'd you make a fool of yourself on TV?"

"Do you really hate your family that much?"

"Is Dougall really as phony as you claim?"

I push through them until I've reached Dougall. "No," I tell them. "Turns out I had it all wrong."

Dougall frowns, rolls his eyes. He's distrusting and wary, and I can't say I blame him.

"Nice try." He makes a face, hocks a loogie that lands just shy of my feet. "But it won't get you that ticket." His face is red, his expression hectic, but there's no doubt he means every word.

"Maybe so," I tell him. "But with or without you, I'm boarding that trolley."

"Good luck with that." He chases the words with a laugh. "You'll be stuck here forever—only now, instead of being an International Superstar, you'll be known as the infamous loser who had everything and threw it away."

His words nail me like a brutal game of dodgeball. It's true that I did have everything, even if it wasn't perfect, and yet I couldn't wait to turn my back on it all so I could come here.

"I was wrong about a lot of things." I angle the board under my foot. "Still, we had some good times, mostly thanks to you."

He screws his mouth to the side, his expression transitioning from hateful to skeptical, which is probably more than I deserve. So without another word I push past him, hoping I'll find my way to the trolley before it's too late.

The paparazzi chase alongside me as a bunch of cars screech to a stop, the drivers all reaching for their cell phones in hopes of capturing a celebrity meltdown in the making. I decide to bail on the board and settle for running instead, hoping for a Christmas miracle that'll send me in the right direction. And once I really get going, my arms and legs pumping, I start to believe I just might pull this thing off. Until my left heel comes down wrong and I'm fighting to keep my balance, my hands windmilling wildly before me, as the photogs close in, capturing every embarrassing moment.

Somewhere nearby, a squeaky horn bleats, followed by a voice shouting, "Move it, losers! Can't you see I'm in a hurry?" I turn and see Plum, cutting off an old bald guy driving a Ferrari as she jumps the curb and sends the crush of photogs running and screaming.

"Why are you just standing there?" She pulls up beside me on Holly's pink Vespa. "I thought you were in a hurry."

It takes a moment to process, but once I do, the next thing I know I'm hopping on the back of the scooter.

"Ezer let me go just after you left, and I found this abandoned outside." Plum gives an affectionate tap to the side mirror. "Apparently Holly didn't like it as much as she pretended on TV. And if she doesn't want it, I figure I might as well keep it."

"You do know it's pink?" I gesture toward her all-black ensemble.

"Yeah. So? Just because I dress like this, you think that makes me antipink?"

I start to say yes but, knowing better than to assume, I swallow it instead.

Seemingly satisfied, she grins and says, "So tell me, Nick Dashaway, where are we going? I assume you found the ticket?"

It doesn't take long for the photogs to regroup and resume taking pics. And when the continuous flash of their bulbs captures Plum's image too, that's when I decide I can't let her do this. It's bad enough they'll ruin Dougall. I can't let them destroy her as well.

I mean, first she gets caught going through Tinsley's purse because of me, and now she's stolen Holly's Vespa in order to help me—all of it documented in a way that'll haunt her for eternity.

It's too much.

I'm grateful, but I can't let her get more involved than she already is.

"What'll it be, Nick? Are we gonna sit here and pose for pictures, or are you going to tell me where you want me to take you?"

She twists around until she's facing me, and ... I don't

really know how to explain it, but when her eyes find mine, my gut does this thing that makes it go all jittery and squiggly, like there's a jellyfish living inside.

I take a deep breath and climb off the bike. "Thanks," I say. "But I think it's better if you leave while you can."

I've put a handful of steps between us when she shouts, "Don't be such a whiny little loser, Nick Dashaway. You want to get out of here or not?"

I do. More than anything, I do.

I turn, a gazillion yeses written all over my face.

"Then get back on the bike and let me worry about the rest. I'm doing a good deed—and isn't that how all angels get their wings?"

For a moment I can't help but wonder if she's serious. But when she laughs, I realize that's just Plum's bizarre sense of humor at work.

"Oh, and you better wear this." She unbuckles the helmet, the *pink* helmet that matches the Vespa, and hands it to me.

"I'm not wearing that!" I push it away.

"Really, Nick? Don't you think it's maybe a little too late to start worrying about your image? Besides, what would you rather do: wear a pink helmet that no one will look twice at or ride around as your highly recognizable self on the back of a pink Vespa? Yours to decide."

Without another word, I dump the helmet onto my head.

After seizing the moment to indulge in a little laugh at

my expense, Plum revs the motor and says, "So, the trolley stop?"

My eyes widen. "How did you know—?" But before I can finish, I say, "Of course! Your mom's friend's cousin Chantal is married to Sparks!"

"How'd you know that?" She squints her eyes and screws her lips to the side. "I don't remember ever telling you that."

"I do." I grin.

"I know because I overheard my mom talking with Sparks. All this time I thought it was just some crazy, made-up story. I'm still not sure I believe it, which is one of the reasons I'm here. Some things you just need to see for yourself."

"Well, if you get me there on time, not only will you get to see it, but you'll also never have to see me again."

"Kinda hard to miss you when your face is plastered just about anywhere a person could look."

Her words stop me cold. I never thought about what happens when I'm gone.

Does this entire world just vanish as though it never existed?

Or does it continue to go on with alternate versions of everyone I know playing their roles?

It's exactly the kind of hypothesis Dougall would love to ponder.

Maybe someday I'll ask him.

She steers the Vespa toward the curb, about to merge onto the street, when Dougall skates up beside us.

6 Minutes and 16 Seconds till Christmas

ALL I WANT FOR CHRISTMAS IS . . .

"Wait!" Dougall shouts, his voice hoarse, out of breath, as he jumps right in front of us, blocking our way. "Just give me a second." He lifts his hands in surrender. "Okay, a few seconds, but that's all, I swear."

I shake my head. I did my best to make things right, but now he's really testing my patience. "If you think you can stop me from getting on that trolley—" I start, but before I can finish, he reaches into his pocket and hands over the ticket.

"Whatever happens from here, I'll deal," he says. "But you should go while you can."

"You! I should've known it was you!" Plum whirls on him in outrage. "You're such a little—"

"It's all right." My gaze meets Dougall's. "We're good. Everything's good." Then, switching to Plum, I say, "You should really cut him a break. Tinsel Hills is a tough town, and true friends are hard to come by."

Dougall shoots a hopeful look at Plum as she rolls her eyes at me and says, "Are you done being all mushy so we can finish this thing?"

When they both laugh, it reminds me of that first day in my kitchen when they made fun of some dumb thing I said. Only this time it doesn't bother me. If it brings them together, it's worth a little fun at my expense.

Dougall moves out of our way. "Good luck, Nick," he says, and this time I can tell that he means it.

Plum charges onto the street and drives like a maniac, weaving in and out of traffic, passing on the right, even using the sidewalks when necessary, anything to beat a red light.

But when a teen driving a white Rolls-Royce with a Christmas wreath attached to the trunk cuts her off at a yellow light, she waves her fist and calls the driver a string of unrepeatable names, then settles in for the wait.

"Sorry, Nick. But we're close, really close, so don't worry."

"I should be the one who's sorry. I—" I try to thank her, try to apologize for all the trouble I've caused, but she waves it away.

"Just tell me one thing." She twists around until she's

facing me. "Is it better there? The place you're going back to—is it so much better than here?"

I take a moment to consider the question. At the very least, I owe her the truth.

"No," I say. "The place itself is neither better nor worse. The thing is, *I'm* better there than I am here."

She studies me for a long while, then places a hand on either side of my helmet and kisses me smack on the lips.

A real kiss.

One that lasts more than three seconds.

One I'm reluctant to end.

"I thought you hated me." I say, eventually pulling away.

"Guess I was wrong about you." She grins. "Also, I figure you deserve to be kissed by a girl who truly wants to kiss you."

Her face grows soft. She lingers in my space. Exhibiting all the signs that she wants to do it again, and believe me, I'm willing, but when the sound of "Jingle Bells" suddenly blares through the street and the trolley stops at the curb just ahead, the moment is lost.

"Go, Nick Dashaway," she whispers in a voice turned suddenly hoarse. "Go—before it's too late!"

Still wearing the helmet, I jump off the Vespa and race toward the trolley, dodging in and out of oncoming traffic and setting off a riot of horns and thinly veiled threats from the motorists. Aware of Plum's muffled voice cheering me on, the shouts of paparazzi chasing behind me, and the asphalt beneath my feet growing increasingly slippery.

First my right toe, then my left, nearly skid out from under me, caught on something wet, squishy, and white.

And that's when I see it.

The impossible manifesting before me.

Despite this being a place of permanent sunshine, the sky is unleashing a torrent of snow that falls so hard and fast it reminds me of the storm in Greentree just five days before.

From somewhere behind me, Plum whoops and hollers, urging me to get up, keep going, as I stumble, unable to gain any traction, my humiliating escape carefully documented by a crush of paparazzi that continues to multiply. I can only imagine the headlines to follow.

None of which will matter if I can just board that trolley.

Running, gasping, falling—I shout at the top of my lungs, begging the driver to stop as the snow begins to pile up all around me. But still I continue well past the point when my legs begin to go numb and my lungs expand so much I'm sure I'll implode. Running toward the life I truly want and away from a dream that never really fit.

With the paparazzi still on my tail, I take a spill so epic it sends me sliding halfway down the street as the trolley shrinks smaller and smaller, fading into the distance.

I drop my head in my hands, unable to watch as my last shred of hope dissolves before me and the paparazzi gather around, taking pictures and shouting my name.

I struggle to my feet, left with no choice but to face an inconceivable future entirely of my making, when my ears fill with the squealing of metal on metal, followed by the repetitive beep of an oversized vehicle backing up, the sound of "Jingle Bells" trilling nearby.

"Heya, kid!" The trolley driver sticks his head out the window, white dreadlocks swinging. "Ya comin' or wha?"

I turn toward the shocked photogs, grinning as I say, "Tell Ezer thanks for the opportunity, but it's time for me to go home."

Stealing a last look at Plum, wanting to savor the memory of her swirling in the snow and waving back at me, I limp toward the bus, heave myself up the steps, and hand over the dirty, crumpled, torn, but hopefully still valid ticket.

"Sorry 'bout that," the driver says, his crazy glasses spiraling in and out as he palms the ticket and shoots me a gap-toothed grin. "Jus' a li'l insurance on my part. Had to make sure you're serious about returnin'."

"Oh, I'm serious," I say, making my weary way toward the last row. "I can't wait to go home."

HOLIDAY DELIVERY

DECEMBER 25 → DECEMBER 19

MAGIC OF THE SEASON

Just like the last time, the snow goes into full-on blizzard mode, slamming the trolley from side to side. The movement makes me so queasy I close my eyes and try to settle into the ride, only to open them again when the trolley comes to a halt. "Careful out there," the driver says. "Big storm's a-comin'. Looks like we'll get that white Christmas after all. If it can hold a week."

A week?

"What day is it?" I heave my bag over my shoulder and make my way down the aisle.

"December nineteenth. Five days to go, so we'll see. Might wanna zip up that hoodie yer wearin'. It's toasty in here, but it's cold out there."

I gaze down at my clothes. My Greentree clothes. Including the Christmas sweater my mom knit for me.

"So it's like it never happened? I won't have to explain anything to my parents?"

He pushes his glasses onto his forehead and peers at me with eyes that nearly disappear between thick layers of bushy white brows and red cheeks. "Course it happened! Everything happens! Only it happens all at once—on all different levels, with all different outcomes. I thought you understood that?"

"Dougall's always been better at understanding that stuff," I say. "Even so, there's only one level, one dimension, and one outcome I'm interested in." I make my way down the steps, pausing a moment to enjoy the feel of my feet firmly planted on Greentree soil.

"Merry Christmas!" the driver calls in a blur of flashing eyes and gold teeth. Shutting the door behind me, he pulls away from the curb and vanishes into the wintry swirl as I make my way down a series of familiar streets piled with snow.

Only instead of hating on it like I usually would, instead of complaining about the long walk from the bus stop and wishing I was on a tropical beach, I take the time to truly appreciate it.

As it turns out, constant sunshine is overrated.

It's only when I've reached Plum's house and notice the soft glow of lights coming from inside that I realize I passed

Tinsley Barnes's and Mac Turtledove's streets a few blocks ago and didn't even notice.

I consider that progress.

When I reach my house, even though I've spent my whole life there, it's kind of like seeing it for the very first time. With the red and green lights hanging from the roof, the oversized candy canes lining the path, the wreath made of holly berries and pine needles hanging from the door, and my dad's old white truck parked in the drive, well, it's pretty much the most beautiful home I've ever seen.

No big iron gate.

No paradise pool.

No oversized flat-screen, weird art, and scary chandeliers that could just as easily kill you.

And I wouldn't have it any other way.

"Hey," my dad calls. "You just getting home?"

"Bus never came, so I walked." I quicken my steps and help him unload his truck.

"That's weird." He swipes a hand across his forehead, keeping the snow from his eyes. "I decided to cut out early. Drove right by the stop and didn't see you. You didn't have to walk, Nick. Why didn't you call me instead?"

I take a deep breath, wishing I could tell him the whole surreal story, but instead I just say, "My phone stopped working."

He looks me over carefully, as though he senses something different. "You sure about that?" He motions toward my bag, where my cell phone chimes from inside. Only instead of the usual ringtone, it's the sound of bells ringing, and when I look at the screen, I gape in complete disbelief.

There's a message from Plum.

The Tinsel Hills Plum.

I know because there's a picture of her, and just under that a message that reads:

> Always remember, Nick, you're never invisible to your true friends.
>
> PS – Thanks for the wings. ☺

"Everything okay?" My dad stares at me for a long, steady moment.

"Yeah." I watch the message fade, and when I go back to retrieve it, it's gone.

Still, I saw it, and that's proof enough for me.

I mean, while I could never explain how any of this stuff works, sometimes it's enough to just know that it does.

"So what do you think—you up to the task?" My dad points toward the tree in the bed of his truck. "Not as big as that last one you helped move, so it should be a cinch."

I know why he says it—he says it for me. So I won't feel like our family, our life, our stuff, pales in the shadow of the Turtledoves.

Like I could ever feel that way again.

"May not be as big," I say, "but it's definitely better."

He tugs on either side of his beanie so it covers his ears. "How do you figure?"

"Well, for starters, the branches lift higher, and the needles are springier. Clearly it's relieved it doesn't have to spend the next two weeks held hostage by the Turtledoves."

My dad grins in a way I haven't seen in a while and grabs hold of the trunk as I lift the tree from the top. The two of us haul it to the door, where Sir Dasher Dashaway waits not so patiently, before entering a house that smells like peppermint candles, freshly baked cookies, and the air freshener we use to mask my dog's farts.

We place the tree in the stand we've used for as long as I can remember, my dad on one side, me on the other, while my mom stands before us, hands on her hips, instructing us which way to tilt it until it's more or less straight, as Holly makes her way down the stairs.

"Your lame friend Dougall called." She scowls at the tree as Sir Dasher Dashaway inches toward it like it's a suspicious intruder he has not yet approved of. "Said you weren't answering your cell. As if that's my problem." She rolls her eyes, trying her best to bait me, but I'm Teflon, and Holly's words no longer stick.

"Dougall's not lame." I drop to my knees and pull Sir Dasher to me, happy to see he's as sweet and funny-looking as I remember him being.

"Yeah, in what universe?" She rolls her eyes again, having no idea what she just said. And once I start laughing, it's nearly impossible to stop. Especially when Sir Dasher

Dashaway gets so worked up he starts barking and farting alongside me.

"As far as I know, just this one," I say, calming down enough to reach for one of the cans of air freshener we keep in every room. "Though that's not to say there aren't others."

My parents glance between us, both of them waiting for the moment Holly and I explode into one of our shouting matches and they'll be forced to break it up. But those days are over.

No matter how hard she tries, Holly can't get to me.

Not after seeing the alternative.

She shakes her head and storms into the kitchen as my mom looks to me and says, "Well, I guess I'll get started." Which normally serves as my cue to start making excuses in an attempt to get out of helping, but this year I'm playing it differently.

"I was thinking I'd help," I say. "If that's okay?"

My parents exchange a questioning look, as though they know something's up but they're not sure just what.

"I was thinking we could even turn it into a tree-trimming party."

"Count me out," Holly says, having returned from the kitchen to glare at me while she gnaws on one of the freshly baked sugar cookies.

"We could make hot chocolate, invite some friends over, and then everyone can help decorate."

"I don't know, Nick." My mom runs a self-conscious hand over her hair. "The house isn't ready for guests. . . ."

"But that's kind of the point. They'll help us get it ready."

"I'm game." My dad slips an arm around my shoulder in a show of solidarity.

"I'm not." Holly scowls. "My friends are on their way over, and trust me, they'll want nothing to do with your lame-o tree-trimming party."

Again I just shrug. Who knew she was so easy to deal with?

★

When Holly's friends see the kitchen counter covered in freshly baked cookies in need of decorating, despite what she predicted, they can't wait to get started.

One of them even referred to it as a supercool edible-art experiment.

"You can't be serious?" Holly says when she sees them fighting over tubes of colored frosting. Then, seeing that they are, she sighs and joins in.

In the den my dad spots my mom on the ladder as she places some of the ornaments near the top of the tree. Their usual worried whispers are now replaced with the sound of reminiscing and laughter, as though they've forgotten all about the back taxes and year-end financials.

Not like those things have gone anywhere. But maybe, just for tonight, those worries can take a backseat.

When the doorbell chimes, I race to answer it, relieved to find Plum and Dougall standing on the stoop, looking exactly the same as I left them, Dougall with his crazy Einstein hair and Plum wearing another one of her mom's Christmas creations, yet to me they've never looked better.

"Nice sweater," I say without a trace of mockery.

"Yours too." Plum grins in a way that makes her eyes go all sparkly, her cheeks flushed and pink, and I can't help but realize how pretty she is.

I study her for a moment, wondering if she has any idea of the chain of events she set off with her magical birthday cupcake, but it's not like I ask.

"I tried calling you." Dougall pushes in front of her. "Did you know there's a blue moon happening soon? Which not only is the very rare event of a second full moon within a calendar month but is also said to act as a portal to other dimensions!"

He waits for me to respond, but my first instinct is to look at Plum, whose face betrays nothing.

"Apparently there are all kinds of rituals to go with it. We'll have to get a hold of some candles and stuff, but how hard can that be? I was thinking we should definitely do it. But first we need to decide where we want to go, because you don't want to end up just anywhere." Then, remembering Plum standing behind him, half outside, half inside, he says, "Oh, you can come too if you want."

Plum looks at me, but I just shake my head. "I don't know," I say. "My mom made cookies, my dad made hot chocolate, we're decorating the tree, and, of course, there's always the appeal of Sir Dasher Dashaway's farting sprees. I can't really think of anywhere I'd rather be."

Dougall's face drops in disappointment.

Plum's face lifts in relief.

And as I lead them inside, I swear I hear Plum whisper, "Welcome home, Nick."

ACKNOWLEDGMENTS

I owe big, huge, sparkly thanks to my editor, Krista Vitola, for her unerring guidance, smarts, and enthusiasm; my agent, Bill Contardi, for being the awesome person he is; my husband, Sandy, for sharing the same idea, at the same time, the second that song came on the radio; and lastly, to the Who, for writing and recording that song.

ABOUT THE AUTHOR

Alyson Noël is the number one *New York Times* bestselling, award-winning author of twenty-three novels, including the series the Immortals, Riley Bloom, the Soul Seekers, and the Beautiful Idols. Born and raised in Orange County, California, she has lived in both Mykonos and Manhattan and is now settled back in Southern California. Visit her at alysonnoel.com.

Follow Alyson on: